SURVIVING VIOLENCE IN A HOSTILE CITY

BOOK II

K S ALAN AND LORNA DARE

ISBN 978-1-965390-55-9 (softcover)
ISBN 978-1-965390-56-6 (ebook)

Printed in the United States of America.

CONTENTS

This book is not politically correct; it is life and death correct!

Your city is in a state of martial law. You look out your window and there is a gang of people coming up your street. They are going house to house stealing and killing anyone who gets in their way. This is not a biker gang or a normal street gang. These are the "good people" of your community who are desperate for food and water. They are joined by the criminal element of your city. The radio has been telling you about the killing and raping and looting. You have your wife and two children with you. You look out the window again, and now they are in front of your house. What are you going to do?

Last year two guys broke into a house and tied the husband up in the basement and then raped and killed his wife and his daughter. Finally, he was able to free himself, but what did he do? He crawled out of a basement window and ran to the neighbor's house! Is that the kind of person you are? Is that the kind of person you will have to become because you don't have the weapons and skills to save your family? No, that is not you!

You step outside with your AR-15. You shoot the leader in the head, and the crowd starts to run. You shoot three others and step back inside. The rest of the gang is gone, and you and your family have survived. How did you do this, because you are lucky? Maybe it's because you are a hunter and can shoot?

No. There is a great deal more to winning a gun battle than just being a good shot. You had to know how to set up your home for defense; your family had to know what action they had to take. You understood the mentality of a mob. You had to have the right weapon, not just a gun. You won because you spent your money on weapons and equipment. You didn't spend most of your free time at the golf course or sitting around watching TV. You spent your free time training for this possibility, which is now reality.

You and your family will survive because of you and your skills, or you and your family will die because of your lack of skills. You don't win gun battles with luck! You win them with superior skill, weapons and tactics.

You must take control of your life and be responsible for yourself and your family to ensure your survival.

This book is about surviving the violence that often comes at the time of a disaster. However, you need those same skills and mindset now before a disaster hits, in your everyday world. There is danger in every city, every day. More U.S. civilians are killed every year in this country than are killed in wars.

I am not sure when or how it happened, but somewhere along the line most people have lost their basic instinct to survive. Thank Heaven our ancestors had that basic instinct or we wouldn't be here today. In the 1800's a man would not have thought of turning over his responsibility for the safety and care of his family to others. If something happened he took care of it himself. There may have only been one law enforcement officer within 50 miles. The husband/father took care of all the family's needs—food, safety and a home.

Today most of us have turned the safety and survival of our family over to someone else. You don't have a gun and you don't train! You will just call the police if something happens. Think about it. Who are you going to call? I don't mean the city police or the sheriff. I mean do you know who you are calling and who is coming? Who are you relying on to save you and your family? Do you know their name? Are they married, old, young, how well trained are they? How often do they shoot, and how good are their skills?

If you hear someone at the back door, see the doorknob turning and realize someone is trying to get in, REMEMBER! When seconds count, the police are only minutes away! They will be there in time to draw the white line around the body and put up the yellow crime scene tape.

What will make the difference for whose body is on the floor will depend on you and your skills and your mindset at that very moment.

Do you want to be the man who crawled out of the window and left his family to die, or are you going to be the man who stepped up and saved his family? Even if you don't realize it, your family is looking to you to take care of them. There are many women out there who are very confident and can handle a weapon and take care of themselves, but still I think most families look to the husband and father to take the lead. If you are in a strange or large city with your wife and twelve year old daughter and two scary guys walk up to you when there is no one else around, what do you think your wife is going to do? Do you think she is going to pull out her phone and call 911? No, she is going to look at you and expect you to take care of her; can you do that?

At Katrina people died from gunshot wounds as well as from the flood, starvation or diseases. Many women were raped, and a man was killed fighting over a dead dog for food to eat. Right after the storm there were gangs of men in groups of 10 to 12 running around many subdivisions. They would surround a home and then break in the windows and doors to steal everything. If people were found at home, the gangs would rape any woman or kill anyone who would resist. Many policemen stayed home to take care of their families.

It's time to start preparing!! You need to learn how to put the bullet in the bad guy's head, or experience what it feels like to be a victim.

This book is going to teach you some skill, but it is not going to make you a navy seal. If you are going to survive then you are going to have to spend money and a lot of time training and I mean a lot of time. But what we can't teach you is one of the most important survival skills. Your training will be of no use to you if you are not willing to act. You are the good guy, your conscience and morals will stand in your way. You must start to think and talk about what you are willing to do to survive. Your survival may not depend on if the other guy will shoot you but will you shoot?

PROLOGUE ~

Categories of Disasters

In this book we are going to teach you how to not only survive, but also combat and overwhelm gangs and looters to survive the violence that accompanies any disaster. You will learn to be the predator, not prey.

The level of violence varies for many reasons, but mostly the longer the disaster lasts the higher the level of violence. To be effective in this and, we need to discuss standard categories of disasters. The duration of a disaster will determine how much food, water and medical supplies you will need.

We checked to see what others were using to classify disasters so we would be consistent with them. We found that in the Government, each agency uses different standards to classify disasters, and most cities use their own categories. Many government agencies use terms like local or regional, major or natural, or man-made. They all seem to assign categories as to the cause or size of the disaster. None of those will be of much help in planning for a disaster. What you need, and how much of anything you need, is determined by how long it will be before help will arrive and how long you will have to survive on your own. It makes little difference what caused the disaster or how wide spread it is, big or little, man-made or natural, you need to know how long you must plan on taking care of yourself.

Listed below are the standard categories of disasters that we will be using throughout the book.

Stage One Disaster:

You will know this disaster is coming, and the authorities will start to make preparations for the disaster prior to it happening.

Events like hurricanes: We know several days before a hurricane hits land, and when and where it will hit. Local, state and federal agencies will be making plans for search and rescue and recovery before the damage happens.

You can expect help to start coming soon after the disaster. There should be shelters to go to and food and water coming within a day or two.

You will most likely only need to have enough supplies to last 3 to 7 days.

Stage Two Disaster:

This is a disaster that happens without any warning but the damage is within the ability of the authorities to start recovery immediately after the disaster, and you should have help within 7 to 14 days.

An example of a stage two disaster is an earthquake. There may be no warning, but the authorities would be able to start recovery efforts right after the earthquake.

You will need the ability to survive for up to 14 days on your own.

Stage Three Disaster:

The main characteristic that makes a disaster a stage three disaster is that you will have to be on your own for 30 to 90 days.

It doesn't make any difference what the cause of the disaster is, natural or man-made, local or widespread, if it causes you to be on your own for 30 to 90 days then it is a stage three disaster.

Stage Four Disaster:

This disaster is one that will force you to be on your own for more than 90 days.

Again it makes no difference what the cause was, only that you are on your own for 90 days or more.

In this book on surviving violence, book one on food storage, and book 3 on survival medicine, and in all our books, we will be using these stages to teach you what, and how much supplies you will need for the different stages of disasters. The longer the duration of the disaster, the more supplies you will need. In some cases you will need different supplies and different skills. Some skills you will only need for certain stages. For instance, in a stage one or two disaster it is not likely you will need or use skills for hunting, trapping, skinning and preparing of animals to eat. You will most likely need those skills in stage 3 or stage 4 disasters.

In this book we are going to be dealing only with the violence associated with a disaster and as it relates to each stage of disaster.

FOREWORD ~

Reality Check

During a disaster you will come into contact with other people. Some of them may be friendly or even helpful, some may not be friendly at all, and some may even be hostile and pose a danger to you. You may or may not need to have contact with others. But if you do, you may need to negotiate with them or trade with them.

This book will teach you how to deal with violence from others. We will assume the only choice you have is to engage in combat and use deadly force. We are not going into how you came to this point or why you need to use deadly force.

We have watched all the shows on TV, read the books and watched the movies about what will happen after a disaster. I am sure you have seen many of them. Some movies or books do a fair job of depicting how things will be, but all of them do a poor job of showing how people will respond to the disaster. We have been all over the world working security after disasters and as Department of Defense contractors in war zones as well as active duty military in war zones. We can tell you without any hesitation that what actually happens during a disaster is not what is depicted in movies or on TV. None of those shows come close to depicting the high level of violence that occurs following a disaster.

In this book we are going to teach you how to deal with the violence that will be out there in the streets. We are not going to teach you how to negotiate or be politically correct. We are going to teach you how to be the predator and not the prey. We are going to teach you how to be **life**

and death correct. We have a lot of real life experience in combat. We have killed many bad guys and are still alive.

These are our recommendations based on our experience and the mission as we see it to be in a city that is confronted by a disaster.

Remember the laws of the land are not suspended during a disaster. If you choose to use deadly force you may be committing a crime and breaking criminal, civil and moral laws. We are not recommending to you when or if you should use deadly force; that is a decision for you to make because you are going to be responsible for your actions.

But if you decide to use deadly force, then you should make sure you are going to win. We are going to teach you what you need to know to engage and win a gun battle. To win is to live, and to lose is to die!

We are going to teach you about **Mindset, Weapons, Gear, and Tactical Operations.** The most important of these is the one that is the hardest to learn and execute. **Mindset! The attitude of a warrior!** This is the most important of everything you need to learn. You can buy gear and weapons and learn to be proficient with them. You can learn tactics, but your mindset is not something we can teach you; we can teach what would be the best action to take and when, but when it comes to deadly force it is not easy for people to use deadly force when it goes against their moral and spiritual upbringing and all or their beliefs. And it should not be easy, but in a disaster you may have to do things that you would never do under normal circumstances to survive and keep your family safe and alive.

From Vietnam to the Gulf War and Iraq, we have taken lives to save others and ourselves. Mindset is everything! All the right weapons and training will not save you if you don't have the will to act.

Let me tell you about Bruce. He is a friend of ours, and he is a very good man. Bruce loves and takes care of his family, works hard, pays his taxes, is a very good person. We hunt and fish and do other outdoor activities together. In the last year Bruce has attended some of our survival and weapons classes. He then bought the weapons and gear he needed to become a warrior. He learned to shoot; he learned when and how to shoot. At one of our classes we were training some policemen on how to defend their homes, and Bruce was there because we were using his land for the class. He also liked to take every opportunity to come out to see what we were teaching and to learn. On this day we were teaching the police officers about not going on the defense, but that they needed to always take the offense to win. I was explaining to them about mindset and how important it was. Bruce was there, and I told the class about Bruce. I told them he had come a long way, had taken this same course and had done well. But I said that I know Bruce, and if he looked out his window and saw a gang out on his front lawn, he would look at this wife and family and tell them to hide. He would grab his AR-15 and stand behind the door in a defensive posture and wait for the gang to come in, hoping he could survive. Bruce stepped up and agreed that this is just what he would do. **Totally wrong!** Later we will teach you why and what the right thing is to do.

One day Bruce came up to me and said he wanted to thank us for the training and how it had helped him. He said it was early in the morning last week and dark outside and he had gone to get his car keys when suddenly without a reason, he heard the garage door open. Surprised by this, he quickly went in and grabbed his 45 and stood there anticipating an intruder. (He would have been better off to grab his AR-15 with 30 rounds in it, Bruce didn't know how many of them there may have been or what weapons they have so always take you biggest and best weapon.) The bad guys know you are going to be scared and hide. Don't let the bad guy guide dictate what you are going to do! He said as he stood there and thought about what we had told him over and over, that he needed to be the predator and not the prey. He said he didn't like how he felt, just standing there and letting someone else make him hide in his own home. He worked his way to the garage door and stepped into the garage ready to engage the closest threat to shoot them until he saw gray matter and then take out whoever would be next, knowing they would not be expecting it. It turned out that no one was there in the dark when he opened the garage door, and then he realized when he had reached for his keys he hit his wife's garage door opener. Nevertheless, he said how much better he felt going on the offensive and being in control of his life. He needed the training, but most of all, he needed the mindset to use his training. He said he felt like a completely different person. He thanked us again.

Mindset, weapons, training. Think about the following scenario as you read it, and then think about it again after you have read this book and had the proper training:

You are 20 days into a disaster and there is no help coming. You are out looking for any supplies you can find because you didn't store food and water and other supplies so you would not have to put yourself in danger trying to find food and supplies You have an AR-15 with ten 30-round magazines.

You look down one street and there is a crowd of about 30 people with baseball bats and sticks standing in your way, so you turn down another street only to find that there is a roadblock made up of both a pickup truck and a car that have been overturned. There are six people behind the roadblock. One man has on a t-shirt and a ball cap, and he has a long barrel pump shotgun. Another person has a bolt-action hunting rifle with a scope. One has a revolver, and another has a lever-action rifle. One has an SKS with a 30-round magazine, and the sixth guy has what looks like a 45 pistol.

Let's say that you need what those people have, or that they are a deadly threat to you. You have to pick which group to engage. Which group would you choose to engage, and how would you engage them? What do you do? What are you thinking?

You see that there are many more of the people who have the baseball bats, and you have an AR-15. If you start shooting and kill a few of them, the others will run off?

The group with firearms will be harder to deal with. The guy with the shotgun will cover a large area; the guy with the SKS has 30 rounds with which to try to shoot you. The guy with the hunting rifle with the scope will kill you from a long range before you can get close to them, and if you get close, the two guys with the revolver and the 45 will shoot you. As you move closer, the guy with the lever-action hunting rifle could possibly kill you.

So, what would you do? Remember that you must engage one of these two groups. Which group will you engage, and how will you go after them?

Read this book and take some classes. Learn what you should do and how to win! Later in this book in the chapter about engaging the enemy, we will go into detail about the above scenario and show you what action you should take.

CHAPTER ONE

Weapons – Gear

Right off I first want to say, I am no one special, just a retired Vietnam combat veteran. I am not the last word on any of this. There are a lot of good people out there that know more then I do, I am sure. Don't just read this book, talk to other people who run schools or veterans. Try to get people who have real life experience and ask them what they think.

The right weapon for the mission: if you ask 20 people what is the best weapon, you will get 20 different answers. There are many good weapons out there. We are not going to take the time to go over the pros and cons of all of them. But you need to have the right weapon for the mission. If you are going deer hunting in Colorado and will be shooting at 300 yards you would not need the same weapon as if you were going deer hunting in Indiana where most shoots are at 100 yards or less. There are many weapons that would do the job in Colorado, 30-06, 270 and many more. It could be a black powder, or bolt action or lever action. This is the same for Indiana: shotgun, rifle, handgun. There are many choices that will do the job. Which one you choose might depend on the cost, or maybe it's what your dad gave you or what someone said was the best. Or maybe it's the only gun you have and can afford. Maybe you chose it just because you like the way it looks or feels and you can shoot it well and hit the target.

The same goes for choosing a weapon for a mission. There are many reasons people pick the weapon they like to use. Some reasons are good and well thought out, but too many people pick a weapon for a mission for the wrong reason. You may choose a weapon because you've seen it on

TV or in a movie. Maybe you have a friend who was in the military and he has everything you can put on a weapon. You can look like a Green Beret with this, or you have a friend who looks like he is on a SWAT team with all his gear. I am not saying there is anything wrong with that, but you are not going to be on a SWAT team. A SWAT team is where 10 guys enter a building going after one or two men who are just trying to get away and survive, and the SWAT has a lot of backup outside. The Special Forces guy has air support and so much more. But your mission will have different requirements as far as weapons go than these people have.

What will your mission be? In a disaster in a city or town your battleground is going to be in and around buildings. If you are taking fire from across the street, how far away is that? Is it the width of the street and the building, or it may be as close as 5 foot as they come in the door, or at most maybe 100 yards. Most of your fighting will be from a few feet to 25 yards. You can't be shooting at someone at a long distant with your bolt action deer rifle with scope and then in an instant pick up your close range weapon as they rush the door.

The next chapter will be on training so we are going to stick to talking about weapons at this point.

We are going to talk about the weapons we use and recommend from our experience. We didn't make those decisions based on shooting two dimensional paper targets that don't move and don't shoot back. We have been around the world in many war zones and have engaged in firefights and gun battles and hand-to-hand knife fights. The following are our recommendations based on our real life experiences:

Which weapon you are going to use make sure it is the one that everyone in you group uses so you can share ammo and magazines!!

Primary Weapon:

The AR-15 in 5.56 is going to be the best weapon for this mission. It has been around for a long time. It has been used since back in the 60's in Vietnam, and we have used it in Iraq and Afghanistan and all over the world. It is not the best weapon for all missions in all places. But we think it is the best choice for this mission. Home and self defense for close quarter combat.

Many companies produce the AR-15: Colt, Armalite, Rock River and others. It comes in many models and has many names. We will keep this simple. AR-15 is generally what they call a semi-auto. The M-16 is the term used to describe the full-auto version that the military uses. There are models that have longer barrels, some with short barrels, some have full stocks, some have collapsible stocks, but the receiver is generally the same for all the models. The main M-16 used by the military is not full-auto anymore; it is a tri burst that will fire 3 rounds at one time when you pull the trigger. Then you have to pull the trigger again to make it fire again. You can purchase an M-16 if you go though the ATF and pay $200 for a stamp, but the weapon will cost a great deal of money, maybe $15,000 to $20,000. We don't recommend you get one; there are many restrictions that go along with it. Also, in all our time in combat there were very few, and I stress very few, times when we fired our weapons on full auto. It is hard to hit the target, and you waste a lot of ammo. Ammo conservation in a gun battle could mean life or death; you have to make every round count, so you can't afford to waste ammo. The best version will be some model of the AR-15. It costs less, from $700 to $1,500, (2025 prices) has less restrictions and you don't need full-auto. I realize a full-auto weapon may be fun to shoot and show your friends, but it is not going to be fun when you are in a gun battle fighting for your life and run out of ammo.

Another factor you need to consider is the length of the weapon. A standard version will come with a 16-inch or longer barrel and a full stock. There is nothing wrong with a full size model; it has a longer range and is easier to aim. It will be more accurate for you. The other model is a shorter version with a collapsible stock. To be legal the barrel must be 16 inches long, but with the shorter barrel and collapsible stock it is easier to carry and handle. Because most of your engagements should be at less than 200 yards, this short version should do a good job for you. In the past the short version was call a CAR (carbine automatic rifle, back in Vietnam). Now most people call this an M4 version, because that is what the military calls their short version now.

Let's talk about the sight on the weapon. Many people like to put long-range scopes on it and go to the range to see how tight a group they can shoot at 200 yards shooting at a paper target that is not moving or firing back when you have all the time you need to take aim and shoot from a steady resting position. Or, some people will attach a laser on their weapon. That may be okay, but it is not realistic at all, not for this mission. In an urban setting your targets will be close to you, maybe across the street or in the next building or in your home. They may even be coming in the front door or moving from building to building, and there will be no time to acquire the target in a scope. What you need is a good set of open sights. Some of the models come with a carry handle and a front sight, and some come as a flat top with a rail to mount a scope and no sights other than what you put on them yourself. If your scope is damaged, or if the halo/red dot dies you have no sights. You can put open iron sights on a rail.

Slings:

You will need a good sling. There are many types out there, and you will have to try some out and pick what is best for you. Most people choose a sling for only one or two reasons—easy to carry and easy to use on a bench rest. Actually, you really don't need a sling on a bench rest. Whichever sling you choose make sure it will work for you in the standing, kneeling and prone positions. Some slings may make it easy to carry your weapon, but when you go down to the prone position you can't bring the weapon up to a firing position. You should also consider whether you could use the weapon with both your right and left hand with the type of sling you have. For example, if your sling is made for the right hand and you are wounded in the right arm, can you return fire left-handed with that sling? Weather considerations: You also need to think about whether you are wearing bulky winter clothing and gloves or hot weather lightweight clothing with no gloves. Obviously this will impact the type of sling you will use, because it will need to be quickly adjustable to accommodate heavier weight clothing. For instance, you may be firing from inside a building and have to leave wearing thicker heavier clothing. Now the sling will not accommodate the additional thickness of your clothing. Vehicle operations: Again the sling will have to adapt to accommodate your ability to engage the enemy while inside a vehicle. At the same time, you may have to exit that vehicle and carry your weapon long distances and fight out in the open. Inside the vehicle you will want the weapon to be close to you and available in a sitting position, whereas once you have exited the vehicle you may need to quickly adjust your sling so that you can now get into the prone position to fire. Long Distance Travel: If you are going to travel a long distance by foot, there may be times when you will want the weapon at the ready in front of you. However, during that same trip you may want to sling the weapon over your back for ease of carry. So the sling needs to be quickly adjustable.

Magazines:

Magazines are important, but many people overlook them, thinking all of them are the same. That is not so. You may have the best AR you can buy, but it is the magazine that will feed the rounds into your weapon. Without rounds in the chamber your weapon is no more than a club, and not a good club. Some people will spend $2,000 on a weapon and then want to buy a $10 magazine to save money. You will need a lot of magazines. You should have 20 or more. Also, remember they do wear out, and the springs get weak. Buy a good magazine. Something to think about! An empty steel magazine weighs about the same as a full aluminum magazine. You should carry all the same magazines. In the dark you may reach and grab an empty steel magazine thinking it is a full aluminum magazine. There is nothing worse than pulling the trigger and finding that your weapon is empty when the enemy is still firing! Remember that there are different size magazines for both the AR and the AK. Bigger is not always best. You can get a hundred-round drum for your AR. This will give you a lot of ammo without reloading, however, you need to consider the weight and the bulkiness of the magazine. This type of magazine is best used when you are in a fixed position and not having to move and shoot at the same time. Even a 30-round magazine can get in the way when you are in the prone position and trying to fire. So make sure that you take into consideration where and how you are going to be firing when you pick the magazine for your AR. As for the AK, it also has a 75-round drum. Again this magazine is heavy and gets in your road when you are trying to maneuver and fire from the ground in the prone position. As many AK's come with under fold stocks, you need to keep in mind that the stock will not fold up with anything larger than a 30-round magazine.

There are other advantages with the AR-15. It is used by our military and many other militaries around the world, and is produced by many companies so there are many parts available. It fires .223 and 5.56 NATO, so there is also lots of ammo available. In addition to this, there are many uppers that will set on the AR platform. We use a 5.7 upper occasionally when we are in Iraq or Afghanistan while we are working security. It makes a short unit for use in a vehicle and has a 50-round magazine. We use a 5.7 pistol, so we have both a rifle and a pistol that fires the same ammo. They also have uppers in 9 MM and 45, 300 blackout and others that will fix on the AR. This way you can have different calibers of weapons and only have to pay for one receiver which is more cost effective than buying many different weapons. By using a single lower, the weapon will feel the same and have the same trigger pull with all of them.

From all the information just given, here are our recommendations to you: **A short version AR-15 with a 16-inch barrel and a collapsible stock**. It can have a carry handle or be a flat top as long as you have a good set of open sights as your primary sighting system. we uses DPMS; and Magpul open sights and an Eotech 512 or a Trijicon, both of which mount on his flat top. But be sure that if you add an electronic sight that you can still use your open sight at all times.

Now you will have to decide what AR-15 to buy. You can purchase an AR-15 for about $800 to $1500. For the person who is buying a weapon for sport, target shooting or hunting, a weapon at the lower end of the price range would be fine. But, like most things are in this world, the higher the price the higher the quality. You can buy an $800 AR-15, and with the proper training you will be able to defend yourself. But this model will have the most basic of the accessories you need. If a person makes their living using his weapon and it is a tool of his trade, then he will want a higher quality weapon with better features. Even if you are not going to use this weapon in your present job you should buy the best one out there so that when the time comes when you need to use it to defend you and your family, your lives will not depend on the cheapest weapon you could buy.

People who use an AR in their job will start with a $1,200 to $1,400 basic AR and then add sights and other accessories to then have about $2,500 in their weapon.

Before you buy an AR it would be worth your time and money to attend a one-day course on the AR. At that time you will be able to try different models of AR-15's. You will fire an $800 AR, a military AR and others. You will never appreciate the differences between them without firing them. Many people have bought an AR and then come to us or other training facilities only to find out that they purchased the wrong one. Then had to live with it or try to sell it, and most of the time that costs them money.

Second Choice:

Our second choice would be an AK-47. This weapon has killed more Americans than any other weapon in the world and is used by most of our enemies around the world. It is sold everywhere in the U.S. It has some good features. It is reliable; we have picked AK's off the ground in Afghanistan that were used against the Russians back in the 80's that have never been cleaned and would still fire. The AK fires a 7.62 X 39 round, and it will punch through a car door. It uses a common round around the world so there is a great deal of ammo out there. You can buy an AK for $600 to $1200. Some of these come with a fold-up stock so they are short and easy to carry. But it is hard to control when you are firing with the stock folded up. It also comes with a large assortment of magazines including 30, 40 or 75-round capacity. The standard AK comes equipped with good fixed open sights that are sufficient for the general firing range of the AK in an urban disaster environment.

It has some disadvantages, however. The safety is on the right side, and you have to take your finger out of the trigger guard to release the safety, if you want to use your shooting hand to move the safety to the firing position; this takes a second or two. However, you can keep your trigger finger in the trigger guard and rotate the weapon ninety degrees and reach under with your left hand to move the safety to the firing position. Both of these methods require more time than the AR to take the weapon off safe. This is not much time when you are hunting, but it can be a lifetime in a gun battle. The bolt doesn't lock back after you fire the last round, so you don't know that your weapon is out of bullets till you pull the trigger again. If you choose to use an AK-47 then you will need to have a lot of training and a great deal of practice. We use the AK when we are in Iraq or Afghanistan and are dressed like the locals and using a local car because an M16 would give us away as Americans. We have lots of experience with the AK, and when we are going to use it in the real world we spend a lot of time shooting and practicing magazine changes. I put a tracer round as the 10th round from the bottom of the magazine so when I see it I know I have 10 rounds left.

Long-Range Rifle:

You don't have to have a long-range rifle if you live in a city, but if you live in the country you may indeed need a long-Range Rifle: if most of your fighting is in an urban area it will be up close and personal. There may be a few times when a sniper rifle would come in handy so that you could start engaging people at a longer distance trying to eliminate the threat before it is "up close and personal". If you choose to have one then you should consider one in 308 caliber. Many of the weapons the military uses take a 308, and there is a great deal of 308 or 7.62 x 51 ammo available. You can get a bolt action with a scope for around $800, but we don't recommend a bolt-action rifle. It will do a good job at long range, but if you have to engage with someone up close, and they are moving in on you, it will be hard to engage them with a bolt-action weapon. If you are going to buy one, then you should purchase a semi-auto. The M14, or an AR-10. There are many of these out there, however, you are going to pay at least twice for these weapons compared to the bolt-action. You want a semi-auto in 308 so that you could use it as a long-range weapon, but you could also use it in close engagements because it is semi and has a 20-round magazine. This is something you could not do with a bolt-action rifle. So a semi-auto 308 could double as both a sniper rifle and a close up weapon, but a bolt-action will not function well as a close engagement weapon because it would be slow reloading and hard to acquire a moving and close target if you are using optical sights. Also, it is hard to keep the target acquired when you trying to operate the bolt on a bolt-action rifle, whereas with a semi-automatic all you have to do is squeeze the trigger and most bolt actions don't hold many rounds.

A note about shotguns: most people think I will have a shot gun in my bedroom, it makes a large pattern, I can't miss and when they hear me pump the shotgun they will run away. None of that is true. You need to shoot at a target at about 10 to 15 feet away and see what the pattern is, it is not going to be what you think. As for pumping a round in the shotgun to scare them, well all that does is tell them where you are and that you have a shotgun that only has a few rounds. They can shoot though the drywall with there AR or AK and kill you before you ever see them.

Handgun:

What is the mission for your handgun? It is a back up when your primary weapon is unavailable. It is easy to carry, and when you are in your compound it is handy to have on your person at all times. When you are on a work detail like cutting wood it is good to have, but it will not replace your rifle. You should never be without your rifle even if you are working. It should be nearby. You should always have at least one man with a rifle with you at the ready at all times if you are out of your compound. I have been in three wars, and I have never been in a handgun battle. The only times I used my handgun was when my rifle was not available or it was not operating. I have never had a time that using a handgun was a better choice than my rifle. Handguns are defensive weapons not offensive. You don't want to get into a gun battle with people with ARs or AKs and you only have a handgun. Real war films!! How many time have you seen people in gun battles using handguns fighting people with ARs or AKs?

If you are going to have handguns then it is imperative that everyone in your group has a weapon that uses the same magazine. We recommend that you use a 1911 style 45 ACP with a single stack magazine. Many companies produce these. They are sold new from $300 to $1,500. Most of the cost is for the name or the collector value. The 45 ACP hits hard, and a shot to the head should end any conflict.

For effectiveness and killing power we carry and recommend using a FN 5.7 x 28 handgun. Unlike any other handgun, including the 45 ACP, we consider this handgun an offensive weapon because of its range and knockdown power. We are comfortable using this handgun at 100 yards as well as point blank range. Kelly has a demonstration video out on Utube showing the 5.7 penetrating a level three vest. Other advantages are, it has a 20-round magazine and no recoil. (This is the weapon used by the soldier at Fort Hood to kill his fellow soldiers.) Also, they make an upper for the AR that will change your AR to a 5.7 X 28, and you can have both a rifle and handgun that fire the 5.7. Although this is our handgun of choice, most of you and your group should consider using the 45 ACP because the 5.7 costs around $1,300, and the magazines are very expensive. The ammo for the 5.7 is going to be harder to find, as well. As the primary concern for handguns is that everybody in the group has the same caliber and the same magazine, it is going to be very difficult for everyone in your group to afford the 5.7 as compared to the 45 ACP.

Knives:

The first thing you need to understand is that to kill with a knife quickly you will need lots of practice. The way you kill with a knife is to make the person bleed out, and that will not happen quickly. It is not the way it's depicted on TV or In the movies I have seen a soldier throw a knife and stick someone in the chest or in the back and they fall down and are dead – not going to happen in real life. Everyone says stab them in the heart, well that is easier said than done. First, they are not going to stand there and let you stab them in the heart, and they may have a knife and will be fighting back and moving. And, the ribcage protects the heart. We have seen people shot in the heart, and yes, they did eventually die but some of them were able to get a shot or more off before they died. In the real cop shows you hear about people being stabbed 10, 20 or 30 times, well that is what it takes to kill someone if you don't sever an artery so they will bleed out. Even if you do, it will take time, sometimes minutes for them to pass out and die and they will be having an adrenaline rush. So they will be fighting back to stay alive and can do a great deal of damage to you or can run away to go for help before they die.

So you need a great deal of practice, and you really need to learn about the human body and where the arteries are, how deep they are and how to get to them with your knife.

Generally, you will need to go in above the artery and slice down and out quickly. Even if you do a good job of this the person you slice is not going to just fall down and die.

A knife is a very personal weapon. Everyone has his or her own idea of what is the best fighting knife. The Green Berets, Seal teams, British Commandos and everyone else like a different type of knife. The answer is that there is not a perfect knife, it needs to be one that will do the job and works for you.

However, we carry different knives for different jobs. The one made for us is a large knife. Bulky to carry but will not only work as a fighting knife but will also chop wood and break windows. We only carry this when we are going to the field in Iraq or on a mission where we may need a heavy knife. This knife will take off an arm in one swing and go though a level-3 vest. But it is not easy to carry.

You should always have one or two knives on you at all times. You need one that is easy to get to and small enough to carry in your pants or pocket and yet one you can strike and kill with quickly. We carry one around our necks; it is a small blade, two to three inches. Something you can get to if you are in a mall or around a crowd of people. Also it must be strong enough and sharp enough to take out a person's jugular vein. You should carry one on you that has at least a 3-inch blade and is very sharp.

If we have a threat in front of us and they are within 6 to 7 feet, it may be faster to take them out with our knives than to try and get our firearms out to engage them. But again you must practice, practice, and practice. You really need to get some training if you are going to engage with a knife.

When it comes to killing, the machete has most likely killed more people than any other knife in the world. It was used to kill 500,000 people in Africa in one tribal war. It is the main weapon used by the people of Haiti. But this is not the knife you need for this mission. You need a knife that will work as a backup weapon. There will be times when you may need to use your knife not only for defense but for offense as well. If you need to take out a guard silently, then maybe a knife should be the weapon. If you come up behind them and put the knife through their neck from right to left with the sharp edge facing out, you need a knife with a sharp edge so when you slice forward it will take out everything, the wind pipe and jugular veins. The person will bleed out quickly and can't yell, but the sound of the blood gushing out can be heard for a long way. There are a thousand good knives out there for all kinds of prices. Before you buy a knife you need to go to a good school and learn how to use a fighting knife and understand what kind you need.

Remember, someone may stab you in the arm or leg or belly many times and you can not only survive but win the fight; it is not how many wounds but where they are that counts, just as in the case of a gun battle. It is how accurate you are, not how many rounds you shoot at them, you can't miss fast enough to win a gunfight.

Bow and Arrows:

You are not going to have much, if any, use for a bow and arrow. During a disaster about the only time you may need a bow and arrow is when you need to kill quietly. If you are hiding, and there is a gang out side and one of them comes into your house to have a look, the sound of a firearm will give you away. This is a situation when a bow and arrow or a knife may be your weapon of choice. There are long bows, recurve bows, compound bows and crossbows and air bows. If you were going to have a bow, then the crossbow or air bow would be the best. Not much practice is required to be as proficient with a crossbow or air bow as with other bows. It will cost more than the others, but it is smaller and easier to carry and handle, requires less practice yet it will kill humans efficiently, quietly and graphically as well as animals for game. When we were in Vietnam it always made us nervous when someone said they were using a bow and arrow. Even if the bow and arrow doesn't kill like a bullet, there is something scary about the thought of an arrow sticking in you and the thought of someone pulling it out. You can go to an archery shop with an indoor range for you to practice. You can buy a bow and arrow and learn to shoot almost anywhere. The difference from shooting for sport or hunting and what you will need to do in a disaster in a city is a matter of mindset. The skills are the same for hunting and killing humans. But you need to have a different mindset when it comes to killing humans. You can learn the skills needed to shoot the bow, but you will have a harder time dealing with and acquiring the mindset that you will need to kill a human with a bow.

I used a compound bow for years to deer hunt, I am not real good and was only good to about 30 yards or so, but did get a lot of deer, then in 2012 I started to use a crossbow and it was good for me to about 50 yards and had a scope and was easy for me to use. In 2017 I started to use the new air bow, it is great, good for me up to 70 yards and it looks and handles like a rifle. Easy to use and carry, uses about 3,000 PSI to shoot the arrow. Cost about $800 plus $200 more for scope and bipod. Can do a 5 in group at 100 yards for me.

CHAPTER TWO

Training

How important is training and practice? It is everything! I have a friend who has a PhD in Aeronautical Engineering. I took a class or two from him in college. If someone asked him something about a plane, he would answer in great detail, and we would know a great deal more than we wanted to know. But when he and I go flying, I fly the plane. I don't remember much from his class, but I took lessons and have spent a lot of time in the plane. He has no experience flying the plane. My point is that knowledge alone is not enough.

Practice is important but only if you are practicing the right things, if you are doing it the wrong way then you will only be getting good at doing it wrong. So you need to be learning from the right people. Picking the right school is as important as practicing what you have learned. You need to go to a school that is not concerned about being politically correct, but being life and death correct. In a school that teaches you what you will need to know for you and your family to survive and win a gun battle. When you are looking at a school you should ask if the instructors have ever been in a gun battle, and if so, do they teach you how they won that battle? You will be fighting from your home and moving, shooting and engaging moving targets and running across your lawn. You'll be shooting in rain and snow wearing winter clothing or shorts in summer, so the instructors need to be teaching you how to shoot under the same conditions as you will be shooting in a disaster. There is no reason to pay to learn techniques and skills that you will not need in order to win a real life gun battle.

Remember that reading this book and this chapter does not count as training! It will give you knowledge, but putting rounds down range is training. Practicing in the rain, cold, snow and shooting at night is what will make you better than the next guy. If you don't do these things the people who we train are going to be the ones to kill you and take whatever you have.

This book is about dealing with violence in a disaster. I will be the first to tell you that I am not the best shot when it comes to sitting and shooting at a paper target; most people are better than I am. But I have been in firefights and have killed people in combat. That was not about getting into a good position, getting a good sight picture and letting some breath out before squeezing the trigger. I can't remember ever seeing a person in my sights during a firefight. Everything happen so quickly, and I was moving, or they were moving, or both of us were moving. So, we are not going to try to teach you how to train for a shooting team. We are going to talk about real engagement with real people trying to kill you.

You need to have the right training for the right mission. If you are going out west to shoot deer at long ranges, then you need to practice for that. You will need the right weapon and scope and learn how to get into position for the shot. If you are on a SWAT team and going to be the first man in the door, you will not need the same weapon or training as the person going out west to hunt deer.

We are not complaining about the training given by most of the schools. Their instructors are well-trained and talented people. However, they have to be politically correct if they are going to stay in business. Most of them are good shots, better than I am. However, I have talked to many of the instructors, and not one of them I have talked to has ever shot anyone or been in a life and death gunfight.

Their training will make you a good shot under the right circumstances. One of the standard things the trainers practice is to draw and shoot two times (double tap). They practice to draw and shoot two times and then holster their weapon. Your muscle memory will take over when you are in a real life and death situation. There was a policeman who had practiced the double tap and then he would put his weapon back in his holster. One day when he was off duty, two men came running out of a store they had just robbed and pointed their weapons at him. He quickly pulled his weapon and put two rounds in one of the men, and then just as he had practiced so often, he then holstered his weapon. The other guy shot and killed him.

In another case a policemen had his wife point a handgun at him, and he practiced taking it away from her until he became very good and very quick at it. One day when he went into a store, an armed man turned and put a handgun in his chest. In just a moment the policeman grabbed the gun and took it away form the man, but then what did he do? He did what he had practiced a hundred times with his wife; he handed it back to the man just like he did with his wife.

I know what you are thinking – I would never do that in a real situation. But you are wrong! That is just what happens in combat or police work. When real things happen, you don't have time to think so you will do just what you have practiced.

Another skill that most schools teach is to draw and double tap to the chest and then up and one to the head. Well, I have shot people in the chest, and then I had to shoot down to hit them in the head. Unlike they teach you, every time I have shot someone in the chest they fell down, not up, and their head was going down.

We have trained many people, some policeman and soldiers. They are all good shots, so they think they are ready for anything. That is the problem. Be it the NRA, police, military or any school, they only teach you how to be a good shots when all circumstances are just right, unlike what happens in a real situation.

Almost everything is done wrong when you practice at any of those schools. The ground is level, most of the time it is concrete. You have your weapon out and ready to go or in a holster that you can get to with ease and most likely not the holster you wear day to day. You most likely will not be using the ammo that you usually carry. The target will be well lit, and you will have hearing protection on so you will not jump at the sound of the weapon going off. You will have time to get into a good position for shooting, and you will be shooting at a two dimensional target that doesn't move. How does that train you for any real gunfight?

The FBI will tell you that most gunfights are at a distance of 9 feet or less. What if you hear someone in your house? Most bad guys don't act alone, so there will most likely be two or more and it will be dark. Now you have to do what? Hope they don't come in where you are? Or are you going to grab your handgun, and in the dark and moving, you are going to have to go and engage two or more intruders at close range? The biggest room in your home may be 18 feet long, and yet you have been practicing at twice that range. Maybe you can tell them to wait there because you have to go out in the lawn to have the same range at which you have been practicing. Also you have never practiced shooting in the dark, but you do have your light, maybe on your gun or maybe in your hand, but of course you have never really practiced shooting in the dark using your light – not until now when you are in a life and death situation.

I have been in firefights, and not once did I have the time to get into a good shooting position. The bad guys didn't stand there like paper targets; they were shooting, moving and hiding.

So if you want to be a good shot under unrealistic conditions, then you can keep on training like you have been. If, however, you want to survive a real gun battle in a disaster, then it is time to start training for a real world situation.

The first thing you need to do is to have the right mindset. If the bad guys want to steal something in your home, they will wait until you are gone. If you are home and someone comes into your home, it is most likely they are there to kill you. They will probably not be alone and will have the biggest and best weapons they can get their hands on. In a disaster, people are going to be irrational, scared, hungry and desperate. There is very little chance you are going to be able to talk them out of attacking and taking what they want.

So, the first thing you need to do is get into your mindset of survival for you and your family. You are either going to be the predator or the prey. If you believe that your fellow man is going to get along with others and share, take care of each other, or if you can't kill to save yourself or others then you need to stop reading this book; it will do you no good.

Your mindset needs to be that you are going to survive at any cost. You need to understand that it is the responsibility of others to have taken the time and money to be prepared to survive in a disaster and that it is not your responsibility to take care of them; your first responsibility is to yourself and your family or group.

Let's define a predator. You are the good guy and a good predator. We are not talking about you being a predator like the movies show, a low life taking advantage of poor helpless people. Think of it as the shepherd with his sheep dog. The predator is the wolf out there trying to kill the little sheep. But the sheep dog is also a predator, only his job is to protect the sheep; his prey is the wolf. That is what your mindset needs to be. You are the sheep dog, and the ruthless gangs and bad guys are the wolves. They will take advantage of everyone. You need to be a predator to them. You are not going to be hunting down helpless people or killing just for gain. But make no mistake, you are going to have to train and be ruthless to survive.

We will talk more about mindset later in the chapter on engaging the enemy. For now we are going to deal with the training you will need to engage the enemy.

First, you need to do more than read this book; your skills and life are going to depend on the number of hours you train and the number of rounds you put down range. Here again is where mindset is what it is all about. If you train enough, it is going to cost you time and money. You are going to need to train in warm weather and cold, rain, snow and shoot at night. None of these things are easy. So, again, mindset! Do you only shoot in good weather and daylight and at a place that is comfortable? If so, then you will most likely be a good shot, but when it comes to a real life gunfight where you may have to engage someone that has trained a lot, you are going to die and die quickly.

The first thing you need to know is how your mind and body interact, what the relationship is between your mind and how your body responds in an emergency.

How you think and respond is related to your heart rate. It is much more complicated than that, but to keep it simple we'll talk about your ability to think and respond as it relates to your heart rate.

As soon as something happens, a loud noise, a gunshot, you almost hit something with your car, hearing bad news, any of these events will cause you body to respond.

In general, if something happened that startles you, even good things also like playing in a game, your body will automatically respond by increasing your heart rate. That is a good thing. Increased heart rate means more energy and oxygen to your brain and muscles. When your heart rate is around 85 and up to 115 beats you are at your peak for performance. You can think and respond to what is going on around you, and you are physically strong. However, when your rate increases to between 115 and 145, your physical attributes increase while your mental capacity decreases. You can grab someone and throw him around or run and move quickly, however, your cognitive ability to formulate a response to the action around you is impaired. You start to get tunnel vision and can't see what is going on around you. At this point you lose your peripheral vision and will be unaware of any threat that is not directly in front of you. Your ability to acquire the target in your sights is greatly impaired. Your hearing capabilities are reduced so you can't hear what people around you are saying. This leaves you vunerable, as you will be unable to hear commands and information from your comrades. At a heart rate of 145 to 180, complex motor skills deteriorate; most likely you will not hear the weapon go off, and when you run out of ammo you will not realize it. You will not be able to think and respond to a threat. You will lose your ability both physically and mentally to perform basic skills like the need to change magazines, and you won't be able to address such things as repairing your weapon if you have a malfunction. You will start to shake, and you will not be about to sight your weapon. If your heart rate gets high enough, over 180 or 200 or more, then it stops pumping more oxygen and starts to pump less. Your heart is pumping so fast that it doesn't have to time for the left ventricle to fill with blood between beats, so it provides less oxygen. At this point the body calls for more oxygen, and the heart beats even faster. This can cause you to go into ventricular fibulation and cause death. This is when muscle memory will be the only thing working. If you don't get your heart rate under control, and it hits 180 you will stop functioning both mentally and physically. Your body starts to shut down; you may wet your pants or vomit. This is when in combat you observe soldiers in the fetal position, just lying there and not able to do anything.

See the chart below:

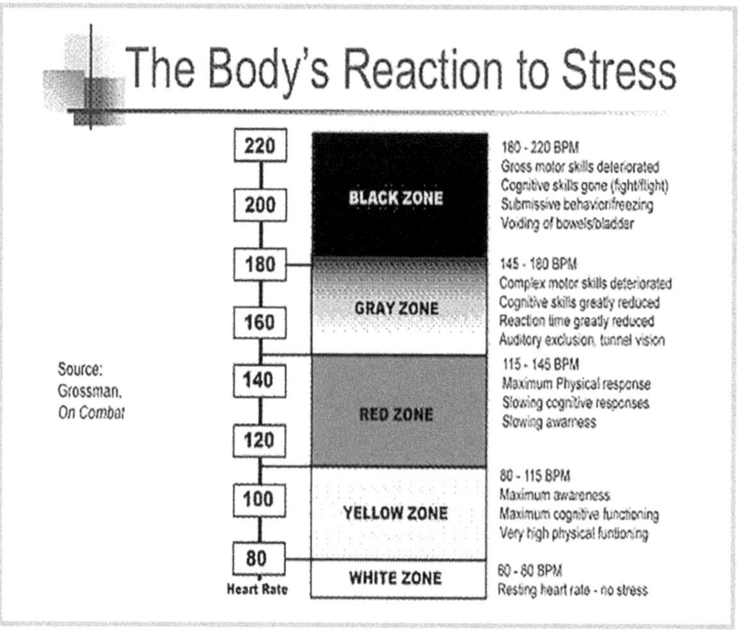

So, how does all this information fit into training? It is everything. The more you train, the less chance there is for your heart rate to get too high. This is known as stress inoculation. The more a person is exposed to the same type of stress, the less the physical response of the body will be to that stress. A soldier's physical response to his first firefight will be different than his response after several engagements. Interviews with soldiers have shown that they had very little memory of their response to their first firefight, however, after engaging several times they not only had a better memory of what had happened, they remembered what they did and what they needed to do. This is the main reason leaders in the military value a soldier with combat experience. So, again, it is important to choose a school that will incorporate into their training stress inoculation. It is also important to understand muscle memory and how it fits into appropriate training and will enhance your ability to win a gun battle.

It is important to understand how your enemy is going to react under stress, too, so study the chart and think about it.

You need realistic training in bad weather, at night, and training that will induce stress and raise your heart rate.

Each time you begin your training, you should get into the same mindset that you are training to have during a real firefight in which you are going to win, knowing that everyone out there should be afraid of you. You are not training to be on the defense, or training to lose. You are always on the offence, and you are always going to win at all costs.

- The only time you should get into a good, steady shooting position is to zero your weapon.
- Your best cover is putting accurate fire on the target. Putting rounds in the bad guys will stop their firing.
- The only shot that counts is the one that hits the target; shooting fast is not the answer, "you can't miss fast enough" to win a gunfight.
- Always train with the weapon, ammo, and gear you will be using for a real encounter.
- Always have the mindset that this is a life and death situation.
- Keep moving; harder to hit a moving target.
- Practice on moving targets; if you can hit a moving target, you win.
- Always be on the offense, not defense; never fight to "not lose." Fight to win!
- Remember when seconds count, the police are only minutes away.
- Keep shooting until you see gray matter.
- Never holster your weapon or take you weapon out of the ready position until all the bad guys are dead.
- Never hesitate.
- Take the first action; don't be forced to react.

When trouble comes there will not be time to learn these life and death skills. You may be a good shot and may have been shooting all your life, but if you can't hit someone who is shooting at you from behind a building and moving from tree to tree or from building to building in the dark, or you can't come out of your bedroom shooting at multiple targets and shoot as you move, then you are not ready for what is to come. This all sounds hard, and it is. But remember you don't have to be as good as a Special Forces soldier; he is probably not who you will be facing. It is going to be all the people running around who have never had any real life training.

I remember when I was in the Rocky Mountains on a trail with a friend and there was a sign that read "remember you don't have to be faster then the bear, you just have to be faster than you partner." That's the way it is with training. You don't have to be better than a Special Forces guy, just better than the people around you. It really won't take much time and training until you will be out-gunning them.

I am going to discuss the type of training you will need. We can't train you in a book. You need to get out there to train and find a place or someone who can train you to survive the times to come, not just make you a good shot. I have killed good shots that couldn't move and shoot at the same time or hit a moving target.

Too many people train with the wrong weapon for the mission. For some reason everyone wants to have their handgun next to them by the bed in case someone comes in at night. If someone is in your home at night you need the biggest weapon you have that holds the most rounds in order to go out and engage them. You don't know what weapon they have. Do you think they brought the smallest weapon they have? No! You should come out of your bedroom with your AR or AK with a 30-round magazine and kill every one of them. Your best chance of winning is to be able to out gun them, and don't forget people don't die in real life like they do in the movies. You need to learn to move and engage multiple targets at close range and shoot them to the ground—not two shots to the chest. That's a good start, but shoot them as they fall to the ground and keep shooting until you see gray matter, never putting you weapon away until you are sure all the threats are dead. So, if you have an AR and have all the accessories on it that can go on it, you might want to rethink that. In an urban combat environment you may have to engage targets from 5 feet to 100 yards. You may have to move from a building to a car or into woods. You may have to shoot someone at the back door and transition to a target 50 feet away in a second. You can't do this with a big scope on your rifle. You will not be able to acquire a moving target at 20 yards closing on you with a 12-power scope. You can't make up for poor shooting skills by practicing with scopes of any kind. The more accessories you have on your weapon the more it weighs and the more things you have on your weapon to catch onto other things as you move.

We all have a big weapon to use to engage anyone in our homes, not our smallest handgun, because we want to win. Lorna has her AR with one in the chamber and a 30-round magazine at the end of her bed under a blanket. She will be coming out of her bedroom ready to kill and win.

To see if you can do this, you need to put up a paper plate and step up to it at 10 feet to see if you can put 5 rounds in the plate in 3 seconds. Then turn and engage another target at 25 yards and do the same. Remember only hits count, not speed. Again, remember that you can't miss fast enough to win a gunfight.

When you are engaging, you need to be moving and shooting, not like most schools teach which is to move to a spot and shoot and then move to another spot and shoot. You need to move and be shooting at the same time.

All your life you have been shooting, and what do you do to be proficient? You get into the same position and have the same sight picture and the same cheek rest and don't breathe. You wait until the sight is on the target and squeeze the trigger. And all this time the paper target is just sitting there waiting for you. As soon as you take that first step and try to shoot, everything you have ever learned goes out the door. Now you have to learn to walk with the bottom half of your body and try to keep the top half moving as little as possible. In between walking and trying to find the target there is only a moment when the weapon is on the target, and that is when you jerk the trigger. Everything you have learned goes out the door, and the only way to learn how to do this correctly is to practice.

No one goes out at night and shoots. However, that is when most bad guys are out, at night. How many people have you heard about who found someone in his or her home or business in the daytime? What if you hear someone in your house and it is 0200 (2 a.m.)? Are you going to turn on the lights so they will know you are coming and can see you? I hope not. So now you are going to have a gunfight in the dark, and that is not the time to try and learn how to shoot in the dark – too late then. You need to go out when it is dark, really dark, and get no more than 20 feet from a paper plate, pull up and fire. The blast of light will kill your night vision, and you will not be able to see the target anymore. You don't need to practice at a range longer than the longest room in your home. You need to practice with the best weapon you have, not the smallest and easiest to carry. Don't use your 45; take your AR or AK. This is no time to be fair. You just need to win and keep your family alive at any cost. You need to go out in the daylight and stand at 10 to 20 feet and shoot at the paper plate. We are no better than you when the blast of light kills our night vision. Learn to pull up and shoot when your weapon is only up to your chest and you are looking over the weapon. Then at night you will not be trying to find the target in the sights, and you will not have to be able to see the sights to shoot.

You can pick someone for training; there are many good people out there. But don't pick someone who just looks good and has a great range. The first thing you should ask the person you want to train you is, "How many gun battles have you been in, and how many people have you killed in gun fights?" It they have never been in a gunfight than everything they know and teach is theory. Your life and the lives of your family members are going to depend on what you learn. Did you learn how to drive a car from someone who had never driven a car?

Going to the best is going to cost you time and money. You want the best to teach you about other things in your life. Nothing you are going to learn in life will be more important than how to defend you family, so learn from the best and you will become the best.

CHAPTER THREE

Profiling—Discriminating

Profiling is a good thing,
profiling is a good thing, profiling is a good thing.

Profiling is important to your safety as it is for everyone's safety. It is an analysis of a person or persons so that you will be prepared for an appropriate response that may be needed. That response may be to do nothing, but it is better to be prepared and not need to respond than it is to need to respond quickly and not be prepared.

It is illegal and unappreciated to discriminate, and everyone knows that. The liberals and press have used both of those terms over and over and interchanged them to confuse everyone into interchanging profiling and discrimination and seeing both as the same evil thing.

They are not the same! You need to get into the mindset that profiling is a good safety tool for you and everyone. You need to think of profiling as an important and good habit to acquire, and you need to practice it and become really good at it; it may save your life some day.

The press would have you believe if you say something that is true about someone or a group, and it is obviously true and a common sense type thing that you are profiling, that it is somehow wrong. Well, you may be profiling but that doesn't make it wrong. Interesting that they never say anything about the people who they support when they profile. President Obama said when talking about the tea party people that they were people clinging to their guns and Bibles. That is profiling, putting a whole group of people into one profile, and it was meant as an insult to all of them and yet the press thought it was great. The President and his people profile all the time. They put people into groups and write general torts about them and use that data when campaigning. The fact is it is profiling, and there is nothing wrong in that. We all do it in some way.

You tell your children not to talk to a stranger; that is good, but it is profiling. You are putting every stranger into the status of being a potential danger to your child. There's nothing wrong with that. If you are on a trip and you stop at a rest stop for a break, you and your family are setting there and you are the only ones at the rest stop when 10 Hells Angels pull up and get off the bikes, what to you do? Because of their appearance and their bikes, do you understand that they are a potential danger to you and your family? There is nothing wrong with you profiling them; it would be remiss of you to not recognize the potential danger. You should be alert or leave or whatever it is that makes you feel safe. I would make sure my weapon was at hand and the safety off, and I would watch them and be prepared to act if I needed to. But this is America, and everyone has the same right to that rest stop including the bikers. I would not discriminate and act unless I was provoked. I will be the first one to tell you, though, that I did profile them and I am sure that they profiled my family and me. Most people that commit crime against people are very good at profiling. Most of them are cowards and will only attack people who they think are easy prey or who they out number. If nothing happens then you have lost nothing by profiling them. Only if you act and discriminate for no other reason than that they were bikers, did you do anything wrong? By profiling and being prepared you kept yourself and your family safe—you did nothing wrong.

People profile every day. When you go for a job interview both you and the person doing the interview are profiling each other, trying to figure out what kind of a person the other is. It is through profiling that people put you into a group that they trust or can count on. We could go on and on, but the point is that we all profile the person that we are meeting for the first time. Within a few minutes you decide what kind of a person they are, if you like them and can trust them and many other characteristics about them. You will be thinking, can I trust him to go somewhere with and be alone with?

The bottom line is that profiling is not bad and is a very useful skill. Profiling is not discriminating! Discriminating is wrong only when it falls into a few categories. You can't use race or religion for a reason not to rent to someone. However, we all discriminate all the time, and others discriminate against us all the time. That is not wrong either. Think about it—someone you know invites you to go somewhere, out for dinner or to a party. You may like this person but you would feel uncomfortable with the kind of other people he associates with. How many times have you turned someone down because you profiled their friends and now you are going to discriminate against them? You may not go. How many times have you invited someone to go somewhere but you didn't want someone they know to come alone? You discriminate every time you go shopping. I will bet there are places you don't shop because of who owns the store or who runs the store. How about the press and the unions telling you not to buy anything unless it is make in the U.S. They want you to discriminate against products produced overseas. But, they feel like they are being discriminated against if you don't support their product.

The truth is that we all profile and discriminate all the time. That is how life is, and for the most part, no one is hurt by us doing it. Remember when President Obama said that the white policeman and his police force were discriminating when they arrested the black friend of the Obama. The president said he didn't even know any of the facts before he said that. That was profiling, out and out. What is the world coming to when stating the truth or a true fact is somehow politically incorrect? How can the truth be bad? Stating a fact or truth doesn't place blame; it's nothing more then the truth.

In the U.S. we use all kinds of tools to try and stop hijackers from getting on our planes, and it costs a lot of time and money and still doesn't work well. The Israelis have never had a hijacking on one of their planes, and they stop it all by profiling. They walk up and down the line of people and talk to them and look into their eyes and watch how they act and stand and move, and no one is discriminated against.

You need to learn how to profile people, and you need to lean how to act so that others will profile you in the way that is beneficial to you. When we were in Iraq and riding up and down the streets, our lives depended on how good we were at profiling and how quickly we could do it. A lot of people in Iraq have weapons, some civilians, some policeman and some soldiers. Just because they were dressed like policemen or soldiers didn't mean they were good guys. Eight CIA operatives were killed in Afghanistan by someone they thought was a good guy. As we drove along, we watched how the people were holding their weapons, how they were standing, how long and in what way did they look at us? Sometimes we only had seconds to make a decision to shoot or not; without profiling we would have died in Iraq.

In a disaster it will be imperative that you can quickly assess people in regard to their intentions, and more importantly to assess their capabilities. It is equally important that you project a profile to others that you want them to have. In some cases you may want the other person or persons to think you are no threat to them. Most of the time you will want the other person to think you are a danger to them and that you are not afraid of them and that they should be afraid of you. This may not only save your life but also save the lives of the other people. If you project a profile that makes them think it would be better for them to walk away, it may save their lives as well as yours.

The bottom line is don't let the liberal press and others put you into a mindset where you lose a very important tool for your survival. You should practice profiling everywhere you go. Watch people and see what kind of clothes they wear and why, will it cover a weapon? Are they right or left handed, important to know because you need to approach them on their weak side. Which hand will they have their weapon in? Do they have long hair? It doesn't have to be really long, just long enough for you to get a hand full. That makes for an easy take down or only a few pounds of pressure to break their neck. Where are they standing and how many friends are with them? How could you use their friends to get in the way as you take them out? There are many things to think about. In a later chapter we will go into close quarter combat. We can't say this enough, in every chapter, the most important thing is your mindset. It you hesitate, you will lose. You must profile, put together a plan and then be ready to act quickly and decisively.

In the first part of the book we set up a scenario. We are going to look at this scenario in some of the chapters and talk about how that chapter and its contents affect the scenario. Then at the end of the book we are going to put together all you have learned and show you how to deal with the situation and win the gun battle. Since this chapter is dealing with profiling we are going to look at the scenario as it pertains to profiling.

Scenario:

You are 20 days into a disaster and there is no help coming. You are out looking for any supplies. You have an AR-15 with ten 30-round magazines.

You look down a street and there is a roadblock made up of a pickup truck and a car that have been overturned. There are six people behind the roadblock. One man has on a t-shirt and a ball cap, and he has a long barrel pump shotgun. Another person has a bolt-action hunting rifle with a scope. Another has a revolver, and one has a lever-action rifle. Another has an SKS with a 30-round magazine, and the sixth guy has what looks like a 45 pistol.

Let's say you need what those people have or they are a deadly threat to you. For whatever reason, you have decided you must engage this group.

To engage or not is up to you and your group. You will have to live with the decision.

We always say that you must never engage with anyone unless it is of vital importance. Remember there is no 911, EMS, hospital or medicines. No matter how good you are, there can always be a lucky shot or a ricochet that can hit you. This is not like John Wayne or Bruce Willis where they just wrap a shirt around the wound and keep going. I was hit in the left hand in Iraq, and it took many doctors and time to heal, and I still lost 40% use of my hand. A small wound can kill you or put you out of action. In our group we have two physicians, a dentist, two nurses and medical supplies. If I get hit, I may survive, but I would be using up valuable medical supplies. I will need help from others and will be using food and water and will not be contributing anything to the group. You can't afford to get hurt, so don't engage unless it is a matter of life and death.

In this case we are going to assume you are going to engage. The first and most important thing before you plan how you are going to engage is to profile them and to make sure they profile you in the manner that is most beneficial to you.

Look at the area; what are the houses like? Is it a middle class or an upper middle class area? These guys may be golfers, or if they have weapons, it may be because they are hunters or sport shooters. They may have someone who was in the military, but not as many people go into the military as they did in the past. They may have been in the Air Force or the Navy. Very few members of the Air Force or Navy use weapons in their day-to-day job. The Army and Marines use weapons more, but even in Iraq only one of every 1,000 soldiers fires his weapon. Very few soldiers keep up their training after they come home, so even if there is a soldier among them he should stand out as a leader or you may know by what weapon he has and how he handles it. In this scenario no one in the group had an AR-15 or anything that a soldier would be used to, so I would say none of those guys are former military.

Now I will profile each one of them as an individual and then profile them as a group. Group dynamics are different than for individuals. The guy in the middle has a t-shirt and a long barreled shotgun. You can bet all of these guys picked what they thought was the best weapon they have, or it is the only weapon they have. I would bet some of them didn't have a weapon, and the weapon they have belongs to one of the other men. They may never have fired it, and will not be proficient with it. The guy with the long barreled shotgun may be a duck hunter, and the shotgun is a pump so it can hold up to six or seven shells, unless it has a duck plug in it. If that's the case it will only have three rounds. He thinks it will spread out and cover a big area, that may be true, but not much knock down power after 25 or more yards, and I intend to engage them between 25 and 50 yards. and I don't see any ammo belt for extra ammo.

The next man has an action rifle with a scope. It may be a 30-06 for deer hunting. But, it is for long range and is made for him to be in a good position to be able to shoot at 300 yards or more. I don't see any ammo belt on him either. I can see by the way he holds the rifle that I don't think he is used to handling it. He will never be able to find me in that scope when I am close and moving.

One guy has a revolver with a short barrel, maybe two inches and the size of maybe a 22 or 357. He will not be able to acquire me in his sights as I move either. The next man has a lever action rifle with a scope on it. It may be a 22, or it maybe a 30-30. Either way he will also have a hard time finding me in the scope at close range and moving. One man has what looks like a 45 pistol. I can tell by the way he is holding the gun that it is something he has around the house for self-defense and is not comfortable with it. The last guy has an SKS with a 30 round magazine; he holds it like he is comfortable with it, but again I don't see any extra ammo. As individuals not one of them should be a problem.

Now let's look at them as a group. They all have different weapons so they can't share ammo or magazines. They don't have vests with extra ammo; it looked like two of them had extra ammo lying on the truck in front of them. They seem confident behind the overturned trucks.

What I have learned is that I need to get close to them to take them out. I need to use their confidence as an armed group against them. Even if I had others with me I would use this approach. If they saw three armed men with military style weapons coming at them they would fire quickly, and we would be engaged in a long-range firefight that may take a long time and might bring others to their help.

Just as important of profiling them is how they will profile me. If I were not alone I would leave the others back and out of sight, but in this case we will consider that I am alone and must engage them by myself. They are going to see me at about 75 yards, too far out to engage them under my terms. I will need to get closer. (if they had the right mindset they would be in a good shape, but they are just good people and they don't really want to kill anyone. If they would have something at 50 yards and have make a rule to stop anyone from coming past that point and if they didn't get down on the ground or stop then they would shoot they might win this fight, but they will not just start shooting someone for coming at them unless they see and or think he is a threat to them and that will get them killed.) I would take a shirt or rag and tie it to my upper leg and have my AR on a sling in front of me pointing at the ground and step out in sight with my hands up and walking with a limp as if I am hurt. I would yell something like, "Hey, can you see me?" You don't want them to think you are trying to sneak up on them. At this point they will see me as a threat to them. However, they will think that no matter what happens, the six of them with guns and behind the truck will over come a single man out in the open. Their mind set is to survive and play defense. They will not shoot until they believe there is a real threat to them. My mindset is to get in close and kill them all in less then a minute. I need to get closer, and when they call to me I will put my hand to my ear like I can't hear them. I will walk toward them limping and with my hands up.

At some point I will hold up my hand so that they will not shoot and turn to my left, keeping my weapon pointing at the ground, I will push the magazine release and with my left hand, pull the magazine out of my weapon, hold it in the air leaving my weapon pointing to the ground so both my hands are in the air. But there will still be a round in the chamber. I would try to move forward until I get to within 25 yards of them. I would yell that it is good to see good people again. Remind them that they are the good guys. They will be asking me what I want. Well, they will be guarding their food, water and fuel and not want to share, so I would tell them I was hurt and just looking for a safe place to get some sleep without worrying about being killed in my sleep and then I will be on my way. You don't want to ask anything of them like food or water, and it will make them feel secure that you trust them with your safety.

At this point all you need to do is get within 25 to 50 yards from them. At first as you approach, they would all be pointing their weapons at you, but now they will have them at the ready, but not with the sights on you. Again, if they let you get this close they believe you can't kill all of them with weapons behind the truck especially with you are out in the open by yourself and carrying your magazine in your hand.

This is how profiling is important to this scenario. In the chapter on training we talked about how training was important to this scenario. We will put profiling, training and tactics together for this scenario in the chapter about engaging the enemy to show you how you can overcome and win the gun battle against those six men by yourself.

CHAPTER FOUR

Defending Your Compound

Let's talk about your compound. This is the place you are going to use as a permanent place to stay during a disaster. This book is for people who live in cities and towns or on a farm. As we talked about in book one, we believe it is best for you to stay in place and not leave. We think there are only two reasons to leave your home in a disaster:

- If the disaster is a natural disaster and it renders your home or compound unfit to live because of the disaster.

- You have a safe place to go that is supplied with all your needs to survive.

We still worry that even if you do have a place you may not be able to get to it in a disaster, and then you are dead because everything you need to survive is there, but you are not. The disaster may leave the road damaged, or if it is an EMP (electromagnetic pulse), your car or truck will not run. People may interfere with you when you try to leave town. The police may have all the roads closed. There is no way to carry all your supplies, food, water, fuel, medical and all the items you will need for yourself and your family or group and take it with you. It will have to be in place, and you will have to get to it. Better to stay in place and make your home a place to survive.

Your compound may be your home or your apartment. We talked in book one about storing food and water and medical supplies in your home or apartment, or farm home. However, in this book we are only going to deal with defending your compound.

We have talked about the weapons you need, the training you need and how to profile. Now it is time to put all of this information together to defend your compound. It is important that you have read and acted on all you have read. You will need all of these things to survive.

We have been all over the world in war zones and natural disasters, and we have never seen one place where violence was not a major part of the disaster. At Katrina, over many of the deaths were by gunshots, and 1,200 women were raped. People were fighting over dead animals to eat, so you need to be in the mindset that you will have to be prepared to use force to stay alive.

Having said that, and having talked about weapons and training and the mindset to be ready to inflict violence on people to survive, let me just say that the last thing we want to do even with all our training and weapons is to engage anyone in a gun battle. Do anything you can to avoid engaging anyone.

Sometimes I have had people say they were glad I was there in case something happens such as someone coming in with a gun because I could deal with them. Most of the time these people don't like my answer. I tell them that the only time I would step in is if my life, or one of the people who is with me, is in danger, would I act. They say what if he had a gun and some other person was in danger, would I do something? The answer is no. My family needs me to take care of them, and that is what I have spent a great deal of time and money and training to do. I am sure if you go by skills, I could deal with almost anyone with a gun, but it only takes one lucky shot, a bullet bounces off the floor or a table and then what? I die, and who is going to take care of my family? For sure not the people I would be defending. I don't have a BMW or go to Paris on vacation. I spend my time training and my money on supplies and ammo. The other people in the restaurant need to take responsibility for their families. The other people in the restaurant have chosen to put the safety of their family in the hands of others such as the police. They drive nice cars and go on expensive vacations rather than train or buy weapons. That's their choice, not my job to risk my life and leave my family unprotected to save them. They chose to put themselves in the danger; it is their responsibility to take care of their family and what happens to them.

This is the same in a disaster, only even more important that you survive. There will be many people depending on you, and you are of no value if you are dead or wounded. You may have superior skills and firepower, but you can still be killed. Many of my friends have died in wars and all were highly skilled. In war I never worried about the bullet with my name on it; it was all those bullets flying around out there that was addressed to who it may concern.

We get sick and tired of people saying, "Well, he was only wounded, not killed." I want to walk up to them and take my AK and ask them where they want me to shoot them, they can pick the spot, and after all it is only being wounded. I have been wounded a few times; let me tell you it is not like what is depicted on TV, and you don't just go on like it is nothing. If you don't think so, just let us know and we will be glad to come and shoot you anywhere you want to show us that it is nothing.

So the main rule is don't engage unless you must. However, if it comes down to it that you must then you need to inflict as much violence on the other person as you can. Use overwhelming force and violence. You must not hesitate or you will die. Remember what General Patton said, "Make the other bastard die for his country."

Let's begin by discussing ways to defend your compound with little or no force or violence. If you live in an apartment building you will have some advantage if the door to your apartment is on an inside hall. You will need to cover the windows so that no one on the outside can see you, or any light or movement.

The first 10 days of a disaster is the most dangerous time to be on the streets. After a week to 10 days, however, everyone will be out of food and water and will be leaving the city to find a shelter or anywhere they think they can find food and water. During the first few days both the normal gangs and gangs of ordinary citizens will be running from building to building hunting for food and water, and they will do whatever it takes to stay alive. So must you. You should throw things into the hallways and make your place appear as though people have been there and left nothing. Don't leave a path in the hallway; get into any apartment near you that has been abandoned and throw their furniture into the hall to try to make the hallway impassable. Try to make the apartment next to you look more appealing to the gang than your place. Stay inside and out of sight and make as little noise as you can. Don't forget that the smell of food will travel a long way and stand out when there is no food around. If you live in the suburbs or in a small town, and you live in a home on a street with others, then you need to do the same thing. Pick a few rooms to live in, break out the windows in the front and throw things on the front lawn. If you have a car and it is sitting outside or in a garage, open the garage door and roll down the windows of the car, leave the trunk open with things falling out of it, have the hood up and a hose hanging out of the gas tank. Use tape and hang wires from under the dash so it appears as though someone has tried to hotwire your car. If you have gas or water in barrels or somewhere, be sure to put labels on the containers that say "danger hazardous material." You need to do the same thing to all the houses near you so it looks as though the whole area was hit, not just your home. This is the best you can do; we have seen this work in towns around the world in war zones. But remember that the smell of food and fuel is hard to cover up and may give you away.

You can't count on this, though, to keep you and your family safe. You must be ready to deal death to anyone who comes to take your supplies. Losing your supplies means your family and friends will either be killed or left to die. When people get hungry they will do anything to get food, and if it is a mother or father whose children are dying, they will be very dangerous. We are presuming that because you bought this book and are reading it, you have decided not to give your supplies to those who failed to provide for their family and that you want to know how to fight and win against the gangs.

Your mindset must be to survive at all costs and do whatever it takes to survive along with your family and friends or the people in your group. That is up to you, but if you are in that mindset then this is how to survive:

First line of defense is to deceive them, next is to scare them off to go to a place that is safer. If you want to scare hungry people away you must be ruthless. It is not just killing someone, but how you kill that is important if you want to scare them. If there is a group of people around your compound, and one or two of them decide they want to see what is inside, then it is important to kill them in a way so that the others in their group will not want any part of you. If one of them came in and you shot him, what would the others outside think? They would have heard the shots and know you are in there, but that is all. They may think they could still come in and take your supplies because there are many of them. So you don't want to just shoot one of them. You want the intruder to scream, and you want the others to have a visual picture that will horrify them. This is where you can shoot the intruder in the eye with an arrow, and he should scream. You would then push him out into the street so the others can see him with an arrow in his eye, protruding out the back of his head. Or, throw acid in his face. Or, you might throw gas on him and set him on fire. Dead is dead, but believe me, the sounds and sight of someone burning will scare the group much more than just hearing a shot and seeing nothing.

I love booby traps. We have used them all over the world, and they work great. Most booby traps are not made to kill. If you kill someone then all the others have to do is get on with whatever they are doing like coming after you. If, however, the booby trap inflicts pain and the person is screaming and bleeding then the others will have to take time and supplies to deal with him. Sometimes it is better to wound someone than to kill them. If the others in the gang have to deal with a wounded person that may give you time to get away or to inflict more violence on them. Booby traps can be anything you can think of that inflict pain on someone. However, you can find military books on booby traps on the web or at gun shows.

Some insight about where to place booby traps: You need to go out and look over your compound. Look at it with the eyes of someone who might want to attack you. Think of how you would approach and what there is for cover. Use this information to set up your booby traps. Be sure to leave an obvious place for them to hide if you fire at them, and that is the place where you should set a booby trap. Have a place where they will have to step over something to proceed, place something large enough so that they will have to shift their weight all on one foot to get over it. That is where you put the booby trap – somewhere so that when they put their foot down, all their weight is on that foot and they can't stop. That is where to make sure there is something to inflict pain on them.

Walk up to your compound and find a place you would kneel down to look. Watch where you would put your knee and hand when you stop to look or hide. This would be the spot to put some type of trap to inflict pain or to make noise so you will be aware they are in that position. That would also be the location to put some kind of explosive charge.

You are only limited by your imagination when it comes to booby traps. Anything that will burn an intruder is great. They will scream, and the pain is so great they can't fight. Even if they survive they will most likely die of infection later, and it will scare the hell out of the others. Remember, you are not just trying to stop the one that is coming in, but you want to scare the others with them so they will not come in.

You should also have booby traps that you can release by hand. There are many types of them, so I will give you the general idea of what I mean. You can then use whatever you can find to make these. You should also have traps that swing down onto people. Those are easy to make. You just need to use something with long sharp spikes, something for a weight and some type of triggering mechanism. The triggering mechanism can be something that they will activate, or if it is in a place where you can see it you can set it up so you can activate the trap. Remember the heavier the trap and the longer the distance it has to travel, the more penetration it will have. Just like a bullet, it is weight times speed that equals energy. Don't forget too that a booby trap that uses the person's own body weight is good. Once a person loses their balance and starts to fall, their momentum times their body weight adds up to a lot of energy when they fall into a trap.

Let's say that your deception didn't work, and someone trying to enter your compound was hurt by a booby trap. Now what? What they will do will depend on how many of them there are, how old they are and how desperate they are as well as whether they are armed and with what, knifes or guns or just clubs.

No matter what they do, you must assume they are going to try to come in and you must be ready to engage them and kill them – and kill them all. Even if they don't attempt to come in, and move on down the street instead, you must go out and engage them. Maybe they don't have the means to attack you, but now they know you are there and that you have food and supplies. So they will be back. They may try to find weapons or come back and burn you out. Maybe they will go and find others to help them. It makes no difference; you must stop them from telling anyone you are there, or in the end they will find enough others to overwhelm and kill you and take all your supplies.

If it is only you and your family or two families or a group you have put together, everyone must be trained in how to use all the weapons and be willing to use them. Your group is only as strong as your weakest person. You must be prepared to defend your compound at all times. You need to keep out of sight as best as you can, but you really need to have people on the top of buildings or out in out posts so you will know if someone is coming. Also, if you have people on roofs or in out posts, then you will have the intruder in a cross fire in a gun battle. We use drones to give us eyes to see all around us with out one of us having to be out there.

When it is time to engage another group you will need to exchange ammo, and this is where it is important that everyone in your group has the same weapons so you can exchange magazines quickly.

We can't tell you in detail how to set up your defenses, because everyone will have a different type of building. If you have a place in mind where you are going to set up, then it is important that you think about how you would attack your compound if you were someone else, and prepare for that.

The most important thing is that you are ready to go on the offense and not sit there on the defense waiting for them to come and get you. You must take the fight to them. If you have paid attention to what we have said, gotten your weapons and done the training, you will be able to engage and overwhelm a force many times the size of your group. Remember, you can now move and shoot at the same time, and they can't. If they can't hit a moving target, they don't have a plan and they will not have the same weapons and ammo; that makes you the superior force even if you are out numbered. We have engaged forces that out numbered us by five or more to one, and those were armies. Remember if they are hungry then that means they have been without food and can't think as clearly as you, and they will not be as physically fit as you are. But they will be desperate, and that makes them dangerous.

You have the weapons, and you have been training. You can profile others and assess their capabilities and intent. You are ahead of them in all things.

Let's say a gang of people has come by your compound, and one of the gang tried to make entry and was hurt by one of your booby traps. They know you are in there, and there are 20 or so of them – men, woman, young and old. They have knives, and a few guns. You count 9 guns, but they are not sure who you are or how many of you there are, and so they take up a position in front of your home. They are calling out for you to come out, or they are going to burn your house down. The truth is that they will want to talk; they will not have a plan and no real organization, just some loud mouth with a gun in charge. What are you going to do?

Because you are a good person your first thought is that you can go out and talk to them and maybe convince them to go away and say you don't have any food or water. This is the last thing you should do. They presume or hope you have something of value to them, and they will be desperate enough to do whatever it takes to get it. They also know whatever you have it is more than what they have. Important!!!! Remember, you can't negotiate with desperate people; they are going to kill you and take what you have no matter what you say. If you go out there and say anything to them they will know you are weak and are afraid of them. Also remember in the chapter on training we talked about when a person's heart rate goes up they can't think, can't hear, and can't be stopped. Just because they are there and you are here, their heart rate is up, and it will not take much for them to charge in as one huge mass. Once they charge their heart rates will be up, and even if you start to shoot them they will not hear or see what is going on. You will only stop them by killing all of them before they get to you, if you are lucky.

You must engage the group before they are charging you; you can't talk them out of this, so this is what you must do.

While the gang is still yelling at you, you and two or three of your group need to walk out the door with your weapons, but not at the ready, If you don't have your weapons pointed at the gang, it will give you a few seconds to get ready before they are ready. They may stop yelling to hear what you are going to say. But don't say anything. As soon as all of you get out the door and in front of them you should put your hand up like you are going to say something to them. That should hold them in place for a moment, but as you are coming out the door you should be watching them to make sure one of them is not going to just start shooting. And you should have had two or more of your people in the building with weapons sighted onto the group to take out anyone who is about to shoot.

Now they are in front of you, don't say anything, there is nothing to say, only something to do. As soon as you get in place you should all pick a target, and it should be the leader and the people with the guns. Using your training you should engage them and kill them quickly. Because their heart rates may not be too high, they will see and hear and recognize what is going on, but in just a matter of seconds their heart rates will be where they can't think. At that point it will be too late for them, and they will not be charging, they will be trying to run. Even if they try to return fire they will not be able to run and shoot at the same time, and they will not be able to shoot well because of their heart rates. If you use your training and keep you heart rate in check, you should be able to kill all of them without losing anyone in your group.

This is the only way to win. If you wait for them to charge, a few of them will make it to you, or if you wait in the building and play defense they will get you in the end. They will burn you out or slowly take you out one at a time.

You must be on the offense. Never, ever be on the defense. You have the weapons, the training, the skills and knowledge to win, but you will lose all your advantages if you go on the defense and don't have the mindset to kill and win.

The gang out there will not expect four people to engage 20, because they wouldn't do that since they don't have the skills and weapons. But you do, so use what you have and take the fight to them, be in control. Never let them be in control of your life or they will take your life.

This is how you will win a gunfight if you have trained; no one can give you those skills, you have to gain them. Remember there will be people like us out there, and you need to train if you are to survive. We will not be out there looking for food or water, because we are prepared. What you don't want to be is one of the people in the gangs out in the street who come upon our compound. That will be the spot where you die.

CHAPTER FIVE

Engaging the Enemy!
Patrolling & Scavenging

If the disaster lasts longer then 30 days you will most likely need to leave your compound to search for supplies, or to look for other people. By the end of 30 days the people around you will be dead, left to find a better place to try to survive or have moved into a government camp.

Whatever the reason, you will be about the only people left in your area along with a few people who may have also been prepared for this disaster. No one else will be around. There will have been a great deal of looting going on in that first 30 days, and you may think there is nothing out there to find. Not true! You will have to look harder and go farther, but there will be resources out there for you to find.

If you have food and water and what you need, why would you want to take the risk of leaving your safe compound and risk being hurt trying to find things that you may not ever need right now? The answer is that if it has been 30 days already, and things are not getting better, then you can bet it is going to be a long time before things get better. You may be where you are for a long time, and if you can go out and find supplies it will lengthen the time your supplies will last and, therefore, how long you can last. Every pound of food you find is a pound of your food you will not use; every pound of meat you get by hunting or fishing will save your food and prolong how long your supplies will last.

Just keep in mind you will be using energy to find things and maybe fuel and other supplies. You may put yourself in danger, so weigh the pros and cons of leaving your compound to go scavenging. There may be other reasons to leave, however. Maybe you have seen others out there, and they endanger your compound. You need to eliminate that threat.

Use the information below to help you decide if you want to leave you compound:

The following information is from ***Surviving a Hostile City, Book I.*** This will give you some ideas on where to go and what to look for when you are out scavenging:

Scavenging is another name for looting. When you are out scavenging for food and water and others come by your place and take your supplies, you will think of them as looters for doing the same thing you are doing. You will not have to resort to high-risk operations to survive if you have enough food storage on hand.

Before you go out, think about how badly you want to do this – are you willing to take a life for food, and are you willing to die trying to get it? Others out there will be!

Within five days from when the crisis occurs, the streets will be full of people hunting for food or looters stealing everything, mostly things they don't need. This is not the time to go into the streets. Stay where you are and live off your food storage until everyone leaves the city.

In Los Angeles and New Orleans films showed people looting and taking things they didn't need to survive, like large TVs. There was no power to run the TV's, but the looters would have taken your life in an instance for a TV that they couldn't use. You will find that after 30 days most people are gone, and there are many things you can use still available to you out there. The looters were all about greed and money. But, remember, you can't eat a TV or cook food with a microwave when there is no power.

Scavenging is a high-risk operation and most of the time will reward you with very little. During the first few days, people will be out trying to find food and supplies. Within a few days there will be no food or water to buy or steal. After three or four days and the people see that no one is going to come and help them, they will start to panic. How long this will take depends on communications. If radio and TV are down and people don't know what is going on, then they will panic very quickly. Personally, as we saw after a hurricane, people soon took everything in a

Wal-mart, not just food and water, but everything, and that was within four days after the hurricane. Soon everything will be gone, the people will have taken things they don't need, hoping to sell them later or have them when the power comes back on.

The longer you can stay off the streets the better off you are. At first there will be looting. Then many will try to leave the city. This is going to be hard, because the streets will be full of cars and people all trying to leave not knowing where they are going, just realizing that they can't stay in the city. If you go into the streets at this point, everyone will be trying to take what you have. After a week or so, most of the people will be out of supplies and will have left the city or be in shelters, if there are any.

Some people will not leave because they think staying there and waiting for help is best. Some will not have a way to leave, and some will just not want to leave their homes. In a short time the only people left in the city will be without food and water and desperate to find it. They will tend to run in gangs, going from building to building or house to house looking for anything they can use. Some will be gangs like you normally think of, but most will be ordinary people who live around you and are now out of food and water. Make no mistake these people will be more dangerous than the regular street gangs. Desperate people will do desperate things to survive. They will leave, or kill each other, or you. Again, this is the worst time for you to be on the streets. **This is another reason having food storage is so important.**

Many of the apartments or homes around you are now yours to use and search for supplies. This is when knowing how to pick a lock is useful. There is much information on the web on how to pick locks, and you can buy a pick set. But I will tell you that you will not do well without some hands-on training. We have picked locks all over the world, and it has often saved our lives. If you can go to a school, again, it would be of great benefit for you to go to an urban survival school. It will teach you lock picking and many other skills.

Places to Search for Food and Supplies ~

Wal-mart, Home Depot and other big box stores:

The looters will have taken most of the food and water from the most obvious places like Wal-mart and grocery stores. Remember, they will take things they don't need like TV's, even when there is no power. They think they can just sit and wait, and someone is going to come and help them and feed them. That is not very likely to happen.

You can still go to Wal-mart and find things you can use. You should have a camp stove to cook, and there will be fuel for that stove because no one will have taken it since most don't have a camp stove. You will find wire and duct tape and things you can use. There will be fishing equipment; just look around for the things you should already have but could use more of. All the stores will have a break room for the employees, so there may be food that was kept there in the back of the store for the employees. Look in the back for the forklifts; many may run off LP gas, so you can use the LP gas tanks for heat and cooking. Don't forget to look for animal food – some would be good enough for you to eat, or you can use it to feed the animals you are raising for food or for bait to trap animals.

Sporting good stores:

The people will have taken the guns and ammo. Hopefully, you won't need that because you already have your weapons and ammo. Again, you will be after things the looters didn't need or take such as camping and cooking fuels. Maybe they will have missed the dehydrated foods in the camping area. Make a list of things you need to hunt and trap and to use in making traps. These are the things you will be looking for and the things looters most likely will have left. Also, look for containers that can hold water.

Hotels:

Most hotels and motels serve at least a breakfast, so somewhere there may be food hidden. These places are also a good source of water. They have large water heaters that can accommodate large numbers of people and many baths at one time. Most of the water in a water heater is good to drink. Remember to boil it or add chemicals if you have any doubt about the water before you drink it. If there is a pool or hot tub, that water is good to use to wash yourself and your cloths, and it is good to use to flush your toilet. There should be a good supply of pillows and blankets. Again, make a list of things you need, and search for them.

Book Stores:

These are not places where most looters will go. But most bookstores today sell soft drinks, chips, coffee, bottled water and snack foods. Or you may need to fix some equipment or create something you need, and after looking for food you can search the "how to" books section.

Schools:

Schools serve lunches and have bottled water. They also have large water heaters. Look in teachers' desks; you may find candy bars and snacks. Check the students' lockers for food and water. School buses are transportation and may have fuel in their tanks.

Self-storage unit:

When a crisis hits, most people will not have had the time or ability to take all the stuff they had out of their storage units. We went through storage units once overseas in a war zone, and we could have filled a truck with the food, weapons, water and supplies we found.

Gas stations:

People will have taken the fuel to flee town and any food and water they see, however, look for food, water and soft drinks in the back of the gas station buildings or above the rooms in the attic areas. If there is no electricity, then no one could get to the gas in the underground tanks. Remember to look at all the places we have talked about to see if there are generators that were for sale or for the owners' use in case of an emergency. If you can find a generator, you can pump the gas or use it for lighting or heat.

Non-food business:

Look for businesses that sell clothing or shoes, or any places where you would not normally think there would be food. Most of these businesses have a break room for the employees, and you might find food and water there. The computer repair shop will have a break room. As you walk around, look at the businesses and think about the break rooms. Look for things you may need in like winter clothes and boots.

Factories:

Factories and large industrial buildings are another important place to search. If they had many employees then they had restrooms and break rooms. These may also have water storage units inside. They may have different types of fuel stored there. They will most likely have animals running around to hunt and trap. Watch where the animals are going to feed – they may lead you to a supply of food.

TV & Radio stations:

Most TV and radio stations are set up to stay on the air during emergencies for long periods of time and should have food and water stored there. They will also have some type of generator for power and fuel to power the generator.

Zoo:

If you have a zoo, you have a good source for protein. Remember, it takes lots of food to feed all the animals in a zoo. They should have food and water stored all around, and almost every animal in the zoo can be eaten.

Auto parts stores:

This is a good place to find batteries for cars and small batteries. These are good for running lights and pumps. This store will have tools, clamps and tape. These are all things you will need, and not as many people will be looting a store like this. If people do loot here they will be taking other things. Remember, there are few liquids for drinking, but anti-freeze and windshield washer are good for cleaning your hands and flushing the stool. more people die of disease than guns in war and disasters Remember to make a list of things you are looking for and take it with you. Look around; you may find things you don't expect to find in a store like this.

Farm supply stores:

These stores are good for many things, animal food, rope, animal traps or things to make traps. There will be tools, and most of these stores will have medicines for animals. Later we will tell you how to use animal medicines to treat humans. Most have antibiotic, the only difference for animals then humans is the amount to use. Look in a PDR and you will find how much to use for humans.

Medicines:

Remember, more people will die from infections and lack of medicines than from lack of food and water or from bullets. You should always be looking for medicines and medical supplies everywhere you go. Hopefully, you will have a good supply in your food storage, and you will not have to risk your life going out into the unsafe streets in search of medicines.

The mobs will have raided all the pharmacies and Wal-Marts and anywhere there are medicines. Many people can't read the labels and won't know what they are looking for. Many of them will be looking for narcotics and painkillers. But, they will take everything and then throw away everything they can't use, or trade it for food and water.

Look in abandoned vehicles, in all buildings and in employee lockers. In homes, look in the bathrooms or anywhere you might put your medicines. You should have a **PDR (physician desk reference)** in your storage. If not, then you will have to scavenge for one. This will give you a picture of every medicine out there and how to use it. Remember that schools have a nurse and medications. Fire stations and sports stadiums or anywhere people come to play sports will have types of medications and medical supplies. Veterinarians will have a great deal of medications that you can use for humans. Gas stations and truck stops will have some types of over-the-counter medications and supplies.

Water:

Waterbeds hold lots of water that you can use if you find one in a house, and other people may not have thought of this. Water heaters are in homes and businesses and factories. Swimming pools will have water. Public pools may have water, but most of the people who are not prepared will only be able to dip out water in pails or buckets and it will be hard to carry. You can use a wagon or a shopping cart that you have fitted with some kind of a water bladder, and with a small battery powed pump you should have found or had in your storage, you can use a battery or battery-powered drill to run the pump.

Look in basements of apartment buildings. When it comes to water, you may have to drink water that you would never have thought about drinking before. It may look dirty, and it may be, but filter it with you shirt, then boil it and add bleach. It may not smell or look good, but it may save your life.

A good source of water is the water that runs off the roofs of buildings. When you are out scavenging for food remember to keep an eye open for containers that will hold water and hoses or pipes or tubs to collect water. Fire trucks have water! Storm drains have water. All the water that falls on a city will end up in the storm drains and then move out of the city. Remove the lids and see where it is going – some drains are big enough to walk through. All the water that runs off the streets and the roofs of the building has to go somewhere. Remember to treat all the water from run off; it will have come in contact with many materials, and some may be toxic.

Unless you have proof and a good reason to believe the disaster is over and government units will be in the area to help people to move back in, don't think of the government units as your friends there to help you. They will be there to round up anyone who is not in their camp, under their control and depenent on them. They will be the enemy! They will be there to disarm you and take your food and supplies for the good of the others. Who are the others? They are all the people who spent their money on vacations and cars and were having a good time while you were spending your money on food, ammo, fuel and medical supplies. Now they will take what you have sacrificed so much for, and they think they know better than you about how to use your resources. "Hi. I am from the government, and I am here to help you." Right! Thanks, but no thanks.

If you believe they are really there to help you, just tell them you are all right and don't want their help and are not going with them. See what they say, and do. They will use force to remove you and take all your supplies, so you need to be ready to engage them and win.

Let's talk about leaving the compound. Anytime anyone leaves for any reason, part of it is patrolling. You should not let anyone leave without a plan and security, even if it is only to go a few yards to pick something up that you can see. If you let someone out of the compound, and there are bad guys out there, they may grab your person and then have an advantage over you. They may try to trade your person for food or medical supplies. So, then what will you do? Obviously, the best thing is to not get into the position in the first place; so don't leave unless it is absolutely necessary.

You have heard that war is hell; well, this will be hell. You need to make sure everyone in your group understands that the safety of the group is more important than one person and that you can't sacrifice supplies or safety of the group to save one person.

It is important that everyone in the group is trained to use all the weapons that are available to the group and that they fully understand that the safety of everyone depends on each of them.

I can't think of a worse situation to be in than to have bad guys have one of your loved ones, and you have to choose between their life and the lives of the group members. You are then in a no win situation. Someone is going to die; the only thing you can hope for is that most of you will survive. Again the use of drones instead of people to look around your safe place is best.

Mindset! Mindset! Mindset!

From the time you started to think about being prepared for a disaster up until now, your most important tool has been and remains to be your mindset. Training, weapons, nothing is move valuable than you having the right mindset. And what is the right mindset? That you are going to do whatever it takes or do whatever you have to, to survive. You are of no help to anyone, your family or friends or group, if you are dead! As time goes by and you are not threatened or in danger, it becomes easy to let your guard down and become complacent. You start to make mistakes. "I am tired and I don't want to gear up and have others come with me to go over and get water like I have done 100 times." That is when you will die; don't forget the longer you have been in the disaster the longer others have been without food and supplies and the more dangerous they will be. Or maybe we will be out there, and you don't want to let us have any advantage more than we already have. We will never have our guard down – never!

So when someone needs to go outside the compound, even if it is only 50 feet, you must be prepared for the worst. The person going out needs to be armed, have communications and take at least two others who have only one job and that is to provide security for you. You can't maintain security and work at the same time. So if you need three people to work, then you need five people for security. Plus you need people in the camp watching and a plan to go get them if something happens. In book one we talked about communications, passwords, food and medical supplies, so we are not going to go into detail about those things here.

Remember, you can't leave anyone out there alive! I bet you think you are tough, but you don't know what you would do to save your child or family member. You will think you can deal with someone to save your child and still survive, but you can't. If you and the others are going to survive then you must think about everyone and not just the one. I can tell you that is not easy.

Remember what Mr. Spock said, "The needs of the many outweigh the needs of the one!"

You are going to be surprised at how many people will survive out there the first 30 days. However, because they were not prepared they will be out roaming around looking for anything, anywhere to keep them alive. Most of those people will not be well armed or organized. In the first week or two there may be some semi-organized groups out there that may have weapons and that is all, because they thought all they would need is a weapon to just go take what they need.

It doesn't make any difference what type of people or group that may come around you need to respond in the same way.

Each day right now we all come in contact with many people with many different relationships to us. Some are friends, relatives, co-workers, church members, or just acquaintances. However, once the shit hits the fan, when I come in contact with someone, I see him or her as only one of two things to me. They are an asset to me, or a liability. I don't care what relationship I had with them before. That was before, and this is now. For years I have told everyone to be prepared; that is what we did, got ready.

I don't care who you are, how old, what sex or anything about you, we only need you if you are an asset to us in some way. Otherwise you are a liability. I have all the dependants I need. To be an asset you need to provide to us more value than you are a liability using up our food and supplies. A Doctor, nurse, communications expert, someone that can contribute more than they use, is an asset. I can't think of any value of having an attorney around. Not only do you not need their knowledge, but most of them sit around, are out of shape and would not even be good for labor to cut and carry wood.

What this means to you is that you need to talk to everyone in your group and decide before the time comes what you are going to do about people who may come to your compound.

We can't tell you what to do, just like we are not prophets and can't tell you what is coming and why you need to be prepared. All we can do is teach you how to be prepared and the skills you will need to survive. It is up to you to decide if you want to survive and how badly you want to survive.

What if four or five people show up after about five days, hungry, tired, no weapons and need food and water and have one of their group who is hurt and sick? What are you going to do? Most of you, being the good people you are, will want to take care of them and give them some food and water and medical supplies. All of that is admirable, but not practical. It is like feeding a stray dog. It will never go away. The people you let in, well or sick also can't go away, because they don't have any place to go. Whoever they are, they had the same opportunities you did to prepare but didn't. They may look helpless now, but are they the people who drove the BMW and went on nice vacations while you and your family went without to store food and water? And what if it was the other way around? Would they give you food and water? Remember what we said; are they an asset or a liability? Will they use up your food, water and supplies and contribute nothing to you? You have picked the people in your group so that each is a value to you and now are you going to make them work for what they get and let those other people sit around doing nothing using up your supplies? Every ounce of food and water they use will be taking valuable supplies away from the members of your group.

It would give you a warm and fuzzy feeling to help them, but then I want you to turn around and look at your child and say, "Well, you are going to die because I just gave away your food. Where is the warm and fuzzy feeling now? Also you need to think about what they will do if you turn them away. They will not just go away and lie down to die any more than you would. You have what they need to survive; they will be back! Think about that.

Now let's say 10 men, a gang of some kind, well armed came and tried to take your supplies. It ended in a gunfight. Well, if you followed this book and had the right weapons, trained hard and were prepared, I will assume you won the gun battle. We would have won. Let's say you killed four of them, and two of them were wounded. Now you have their wounded in your compound, and the other four ran off. What are you going to do with the wounded and the ones who got away? First think of what they would have done to you and your group if they had won the gun battle. You would be dead, and they would have your supplies or they would be raping your wife or daughter. It is important for you to survive! Important for not only you, but for the country. The good people need to survive to provide the basis for the future of the country.

So, what do you do? The wounded ones are not a problem. I remember when I was in Vietnam and out with some South Vietnamese, and we got into a firefight. One was still alive, and they were going to shoot him. I said you couldn't do that! They said okay he is yours; you feed him and take care of him because we are going. After a few days I changed my mind about him. You cannot afford to use your food, water and for sure you can't use medical supplies for them that may keep you alive later. Simple, just kill them.

What about the ones who ran away? You can't let them live! They will come back, and they may find more people to bring with them. You can't fight everyone. You must pursue them and quickly! You need to have a plan in place so you can react quickly. Every minute counts, don't give them time to rest, regroup or get too far away.

Remember you must never leave your compound undefended. You are pursuing them to keep your people safe, so it will not do you any good to pursue them and come back to your compound and find everyone dead. You need to have a rapid reaction force ready to respond quickly. This is where booby traps will help defend your compound while you are out of it.

Those guys will be tired and scared and trying to stay alive and get away, but it is unlikely that they will have communication. Most likely they will not have a back up plan to cover this, so they will be confused and unorganized. At best they may have said something like, "If something happens, we'll meet at a place we've picked." Most likely they will try to find each other and think of something to do; first, they will just try to be safe, and then they will think about how to come back and kill you and take what you have. They will be worried you will come after them, and for all of these reasons they will be very dangerous.

You are going out there to keep your family safe, and whether they live or die will depend on your skills and ability to find and terminate the threat. This is where your training will save you. Make sure everyone has the same weapons, at least 10 magazines, and body armor, if you have it. This is also where communications are so important. In Libya the people were fighting Kadhafi's troops and having communication problems. The U.S. is not sending troops, but they did send four Special Ops guys just to provide communications. Being able to communicate with each other and coordinate plans changed things. So, the power changed, not by numbers of fighters, but because of communication. In this same way, you need communications with your camp as well as with each other. (Book one went into detail about communications.)

We can't tell you in detail how to pursue those guys, because weather, time of day, how many they have in their group, the skill of your men and so many other factors will dictate the details of how this operation will proceed. You can't read this book and shoot a little and think you are a Green Beret. You need to train hard, harder than the people who will be attacking you, or you will lose. You can't read a book on army basic training and then think you have now been through army basic training.

We will give you principles and guides for what you need to know, and you will have to train, think and implement the mission on the spot. Some of the things will sound like a conflict, but they are not. You will need to move and close on the group as fast as you can before they can get away. But at the same time, you have to move slowly so that you have security. How fast you can move will be a factor of weather, daylight and many other circumstances. It will be up to you how to do this. You will need someone out in front (point man). Don't let them get out of your sight; if you lose sight of them you cannot engage and fire not knowing where everyone is. Also, it is better to use hand signals rather than voice, and you can't do that if you can't see your people. Use overwhelming fire power; don't turn this into a fair fight. Don't surround them. If you are in a circle, you will be shooting at each other. If you miss, one of your men across from you may be hit.

Observe the bad guys and try to find them altogether before you shoot. If you can find all the bad guys together, then follow one of them because he may take you to the others. You must, for the safety of the others in your group, kill all the bad guys, or they will return and kill you. Make sure you take all of their supplies and equipment. I would not bury the dead if I were you; I would leave them for others who might come along to see, and hopefully this will scare them away.

You will have to deal with the details of how you make this happen. The only thing to remember is that you must stop the bad guys from getting away and returning, maybe with more and better firepower.

There is a great deal to learn about patrolling and engaging someone, and you cannot learn it all from reading a book or training on your own. It is important to read and understand, and important to practice, but you need to take training from someone who has been in a gun battle. Try to find someone. If you and your group and family are to survive an attack, you must be able to deal out death quickly and effectively.

Let's say the time has come for you to go scavaging. We are now going to go back to the scenario that was in the chapter on profiling.

Scenario:

You are 20 days into a disaster, and there is no help coming. You are out looking for any supplies you can find. You have an AR-15 with ten 30-round magazines.

You look down a street, and there is a roadblock made up of a pickup truck and a car that have been overturned. There are six people behind the roadblock. One man has on a tee shirt and a ball cap, and he has a long-barrel pump shotgun. Another person has a bolt-action hunting rifle with a scope. Another has a revolver, and one has a lever-action rifle. Another has an SKS with a 30-round magazine, and the sixth guy has what looks like a 45 pistol.

Let's say you need what those people have, or they are a deadly threat to you. For whatever reason, you have decided you must engage this group.

To engage or not is up to you and your group. You will have to live with the decision.

We say that you must never engage with anyone unless it is of vital importance. Remember there is no 911, EMS, hospital or medicines. No matter how good you are there can always be a lucky shot or a ricochet that can hit you. This is not like a John Wayne or Bruce Willis movie where they just wrap a shirt around the wound and keep going. I was hit in the left hand in Iraq, and it took doctors and time to heal. I still lost 40% use of my hand. A small wound can kill you or put you out of action. In our group we have two physicians, a dentist, two nurses and medical supplies. If I get hit, I may survive, but I would be using up valuable medical supplies. I will need help from others and will be using food and water and will not be contributing anything to the group during that time. You can't afford to get hurt, so don't engage unless it is a matter of life and death.

In this case we are going to assume you are going to engage. The first and most important thing before you plan how you are going to engage is to profile the people in the gang and make sure they profile you in the manner that you want them to.

Look at the area; what are the houses like? Is it a middleclass or an upper middleclass area? These guys may be golfers, or if they have weapons, it may be because they are hunters or sport shooters. They may have someone who was in the military, but not as many people go into the military as did in the past. These people may have been in the Air Force or the Navy. Very few members of the Air Force or Navy use weapons in their day-to-day job. The Army and Marines use weapons more, but even in Iraq only one of every 1,000 soldiers fires his weapon. Very few soldiers keep up their training after they come home, so if there is a soldier among them he should stand out as a leader. Or you may know by what weapon he has and how he handles it. In this scenario no one in the group had an AR-15 or anything that a soldier would be used to, so I would say none of these guys are former military.

Now I will profile each one of them as an individual and then profile them as a group. Group dramatics are different than for individuals. The guy in the middle has a tee shirt and a long-barreled shotgun. You can bet all of these guys picked what they thought was the best weapon they had, or it is the only weapon they had. I would bet some of them didn't have a weapon, and the weapon they have belongs to one of the other men. They may never have fired it, and will not be proficient with it. The guy with the long-barreled shotgun may be a duck hunter, and the shotgun is a pump, so it can hold up to six or seven shells unless there is a duck plug in it. If that's the case it will only have three rounds. The guy with this weapon thinks it will spread out and cover a large area, and that may be true but not with much "knock down" power after 25 or more yards. I intend to engage them between 25 and 50 yards. I don't see any ammo belt for extra ammo.

The next man has an lever action rifle with a scope. It may be a 30-06 for deer hunting. But, this is for long range and he needs to be in a good position to be able to shoot at 300 yards or more. I don't see any ammo belt for him either. I can see by the way he holds the rifle that it doesn't look like he is used to handling it. He will never be able to find me in a scope when I am close and moving.

One guy has a revolver with a short barrel, maybe two inches and the size of maybe a 357. He will not be able to acquire me in his sights as I move either. The next man has a lever-action rifle with a scope on it. It may be a 22, or it may be a 30-30. Either way he will also have a hard time finding me in the scope at close range and moving. One man has what looks like a 45 pistol. I can tell by the way he is holding the gun that it is something he has around the house for self-defense and is not comfortable with it. The last guy has an SKS with a 30-round magazine; he holds it as though he is comfortable with it, but again I don't see any extra ammo. As individuals, not one of them should be a problem.

Now let's look at them as a group. They all have different weapons so they can't share ammo or magazines. They don't have vests with extra ammo; it looked like two of them had extra ammo lying on the truck in front of them. They seem confident behind the overturned trucks.

What I have learned is that I need to get close to them to take them out. I need to use their confidence as an armed group against them.

Even if I had others with me I would use this approach. If they saw three armed men with military style weapons coming at them they would fire quickly, and we would be engaged in a long-range firefight that may take a long time and might bring others to their aid.

Just as important as profiling them is how they will profile me. If I were not alone I would leave the others back and out of sight, but in this case we will consider that I am alone and must engage them by myself. They are going to see me at about 75 yards, too far out to engage them under my terms. I will need to get closer. I would take a shirt or rag and tie it to my upper leg and have my AR on a sling in front of me pointing at the ground. I would step out in sight with my hands up and walking with a limp as if I am hurt. I would yell something like "Hey, can you see me?" You don't want them to think you are trying to sneak up on them. At this point they will see me as a threat to them. However, they will think that no matter what happens, the six of them with guns and behind the truck will overcome a single man out in the open. Their mindset is to survive and play defense. They will not shoot until they believe there is a real threat to them. My mindset is to get in close and kill them all in about 30 seconds. I need to get closer, and when they call to me I will put my hand to my ear like I can't hear them. I will walk toward them limping with my hands up.

At some point I will hold up my hand higher so that they will not shoot, and I will turn to my left, keeping my weapon pointing at the ground. I will push the magazine release and with my left hand, pull the magazine out of my weapon, hold it in the air leaving my weapon pointing to the ground so both my hands are in the air. However there will still be a round in the chamber. I will try to move forward until I get to within 25 yards of them. I will yell that it is good to see good people again. Remind them that they are the good guys. They will be asking me what I want. They, of course, will be guarding their food, water and fuel and not want to share, so I will tell them I was hurt and just looking for a safe place to get some sleep without worrying about being killed in my sleep and will then be on my way. You don't want to ask anything of them like food or water, and it will make them feel secure that you trust them with your safety.

At this point all you need to do is get within 25 to 50 yards from them. At first as you approach, they will all be pointing their weapons at you, but now they should only have them at the ready, but not with the sights on you. Again, if they let you get this close they believe you can't kill all of them with weapons behind the truck, especially with you out in the open by yourself and carrying your magazine in your hand. This is how profiling is important to this scenario. In the chapter on training we talked about how training was important to this scenario. We will now put profiling, training and tactics together for this scenario to show you how you can overcome and win the gun battle against those six men by yourself.

If you would ask any 50 people who is going to win this gun battle with you out in the open against six armed men behind a barrier, all 50 would say the six men and that the guy in the open will die. They are wrong, but it is good that they think this; because the six armed men will believe the same thing and that will also give you an advantage.

If this group had put a rock or something out in front of them at 50 yards and agreed that they would not let anyone come past that 50 yard marker even if they know the person, make them lay down and go get them and take their weapons or shot them if they pass that 50 yard mark they would be safe but because they are good people they don't want to shoot till the other guy shoots and that is going to get them killed.

This is where your mindset and training will save the day. We talked about how important it is to be able to shoot a moving target and to be able to move and shoot at the same time. Except for maybe a duck or a deer on the run, none of those guys will have any skills at shooting at a moving target. It is for sure they probably have no practice shooting at a moving target when someone is shooting at them.

You need to turn their advantage into your advantage, and the vehicles they are hiding behind can be to your advantage if you do this right.

You need to quickly pull your weapon up and insert the magazine into it as you start to move at a 45-degree angle to their right, harder for them to shoot to their right then to their left. You pull up and shoot the person who is the most open target as you are moving. As soon as that first round goes off all their heart rates will jump to over 150 beats.

Now they can't think clearly, can't see to find you in their sights, they will be shaking and ducking to get out of the line of fire. You should be walking, not running, and shooting at the same time. If you can't see them, they can't see you. You should be able to keep them from returning fire effectively. What you need to do is get to the right end of the vehicles. A few moments ago you were out in front with no cover, and all of them had you as a target. Now they are in a line in front of you, and they will have to move to be able to see you. The others will be in their line of fire, so they can't all shoot at you at the same time. By this time you should have been able to kill two or more of them. The guy with the deer rifle and scope can't find you in a scope at this range as you are moving, and they will all be moving and trying to find cover or to just get out of there. But for whatever reason, by this time they will be trying to survive, and the only thing that is a threat to you is a lucky shot or a round that may bounce off something and hit you. With all of them in a line in front of you, it is time to acquire a target and fire. They will see their friends being killed so their heart rates will increase even more until they will be in a total panic. You will be able to close on them and kill them. Some may even have run away. But you should have accomplished all this in 20 seconds or less. Remember to keep shooting until you see gray matter, and never get out of the ready position.

Whether you are going to be the predator or the prey, and whether you and your group are going to survive, will depend on your mindset. That is the most important weapon you have and will give you a great advantage over everyone else…**except for us of course!**

If someone would tell me there are 6 of them and only one of me, I would tell them, well then they should have had more men to have a fair fight.

When I was in Vietnam we didn't like going into this one valley because it was so deadly. Our leader would take point, being the first man out front and on the back of his Flack vest so we could all see was, yea though I walk through the valley of the shadow of death I will fear no evil for I am the meanest bastard in the valley!!

That is the mindset you will need to survive!!

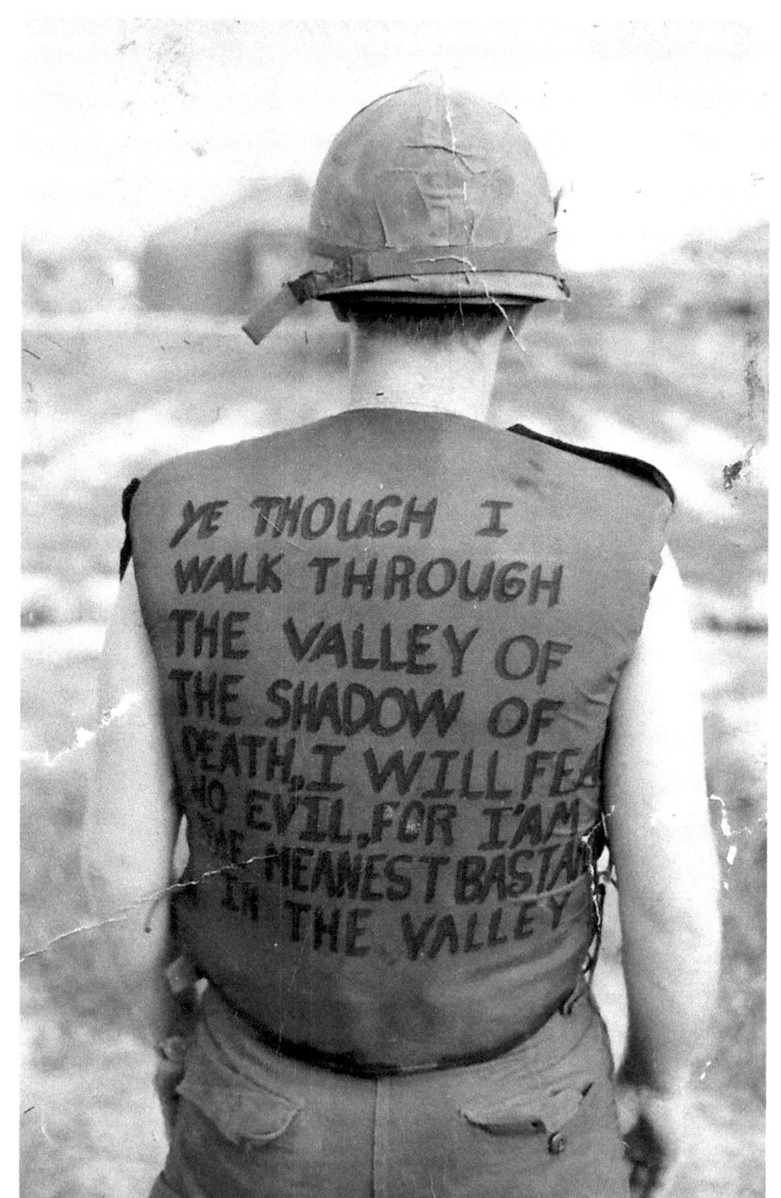
YE THOUGH I
WALK THROUGH
THE VALLEY OF
THE SHADOW OF
DEATH, I WILL FEA
NO EVIL, FOR I'AM
THE MEANEST BASTAR
IN THE VALLEY